Sneaky Snow White

Sneaky Snow White
Copyright © 2016 by Anita Valle
All rights reserved.

No part of this book may be used or reproduced in any manner whatsoever without written permission of the author except in the case of brief quotations embodied in critical articles and reviews. For information, e-mail the author at anitavalleart@yahoo.com

Cover art by Anita Valle
http://www.anitavalleart.com

ISBN-13: 978-1438258775
ISBN-10: 1438258771

Printed in the USA
First Edition, May 2016

Sneaky Snow White

by Anita Valle

www.anitavalleart.com

Prologue

Cinderella killed my father.

I don't know how she did it. But he's gone. Not even a body to bury. When I ask her, she simply laughs and says he got what he deserved. She thinks she can do anything because she is queen.

And my stepmother.

I can't bring back my father. But I can avenge his death. Although my skin is white as snow, my soul is far from pure. I will make Cinderella suffer for her sins.

Sure as my name is Snow White.

Chapter 1

Cinderella summons me to the throne room.

She's sitting on a throne made of solid crystal. I'm not even kidding - a cold, hard rock, the most uncomfortable chair your rump will ever meet. I can't imagine where she got it.

"Hello, Snowy," she says. Her voice billows out in the empty room, soars up to the cavernous ceiling. There's nothing here except her throne and the bare, black marble floor, threaded with veins of white.

"What do you want?" I whine. Most of the time Old Cinders leaves me alone. She only calls for me when she wants something stupid.

Cinderella looks at me with her beautiful ice-blue eyes. "I need you to find me a fairy."

See what I mean?

"A fairy!" I cry, spreading my arms. "Are you crazy? They don't exist!"

She smiles. "Oh, but they do. I had one once."

"You had a fairy...."

"Yes, she was my godmother."

Oh man, she's *really* lost it. "Well, assuming I could find one, what do you want with a fairy?"

Cinderella lays a hand on her belly. It bulges like she's got a melon stuffed inside her black dress. "I want one for the baby. To watch over it."

The baby. Unbelievable. Seven years of marriage without any children and now one decides to show up. The kingdom rejoiced when Cinderella made her announcement. My father looked pleased and proud. For a month, the two of them stopped fighting, they even seemed *happy* together. I thought we were finally becoming a family.

And then Cinderella killed my father.

I sigh. "How am I supposed to find a fairy?"

"Go into The Wood," she says. "And place yourself in some kind of peril. Walk along a precipice or hunt an animal larger than you. Fairies enjoy saving people in danger."

I stare at her. "You want me to risk *my life?*"

"If you don't mind."

Witch! I wish the kingdom could see her for what she is, selfish and evil and crazy. But somehow she's bewitched them all. They adore their blooming twenty-four-year-old queen, with her luxurious gold hair and seductive smile. Shouldn't the creepy black dresses tip them off just a little?

I fold my arms. "Well, maybe I don't feel like dying today. Find your own fairy if it's so important to you."

Cinderella lifts a single eyebrow. "You will do as I say, Snow White."

"Really? Or what?"

"Or I will take you to The Mirror."

My stomach goes cold. No, she wouldn't do that to me. Not again....

"Fine," I say, my voice weaker. "I'll go."

Chapter 2

A friggin' fairy.

How am I supposed to find one? And what do I do if I do? Take it home in a basket?

I leave the palace by the front door and walk down the white marble stairs. They are round, like a series of half-moons that grow wider as you go down. It was these stupid steps that made Cinderella the queen. She was leaving a ball one night and she lost her shoe right here. My father used it to find her.

I never knew what he saw in her.

The Wood surrounds the palace and spreads out, dense and flat, for miles. It is said to be enchanted but I always found it pretty ordinary. I wouldn't believe in magic at all if it wasn't for Cinderella and her demon mirror.

The hem of my dress crackles over the fallen leaves of early autumn. I like to wear white dresses with big skirts. My hair I do absolutely nothing with, it's raven-black and just spills right down to my waist. I might be pretty but I don't really care.

After ten minutes of walking, I reach the well. It's old – the roof and pulley are gone – and the stones have crumbled down on one side. It sits in a sunny grove surrounded by apple trees. Hunter is waiting for me on the good side of the well. Another reason I was so annoyed with Cinderella, she made me late. Hunter and I meet here every day at noon.

"You look pouty," he says, grinning. The grin shoots golden joy right through me. I rush into his arms and squeeze him hard. Then I tilt back my face so he can kiss me. The touch of his lips is pure magic, a spell that melts through my body. He has kissed no other girl but me.

"You won't believe this," I say, hopping up to sit on the well. Hunter sits beside me, wrapping an arm around my shoulders. I tell him about the crazy quest Cinderella gave me, but all the while I'm gazing at his wonderful face, his dark hair and eyes, the gentle cut of his profile. Hunter is nineteen, a woodsman, and the sweetest boy I've ever known. I adore him, I can't help it.

"A fairy," he says quietly.

"I know, it's ridiculous."

"No.... I've seen a few."

"You've seen *fairies?*"

"Just flickers and shadows, they don't like to be seen. But when you walk around The Wood as much as I do... you see things."

"But how do we catch one? Old Cinders says I have to put myself in peril and a fairy will come to save me."

Hunter smiles. "I could push you into the well, if you like." He grabs my arm suddenly, like he's going to do it, and I squeal and laugh out loud. He's so adorable!

"I think," Hunter says, "that the real question is, why does the queen want a fairy?"

"Oh, she told me that. She wants it to protect the baby."

"Really? Why does the baby need protection?"

"Oh, I don't know. She's crazy."

Hunter shakes his head. "No.... She has her reasons. She's just not telling them to you. Does she seem happy about the baby?"

I scowl and cross my ankles beneath my billowy white skirt. "She does, actually. My father did too. They were talking nicely about it. And then...." I clamp my teeth together.

Hunter pulls me in and kisses the top of my cheek. "We don't know for certain."

I shake my head. "It was her. She *hated* my father. Cinderella loves nothing but... herself." Ugh, I almost said "The Mirror." Hunter doesn't know about The Mirror. And I try not to think about it.

"Have you ever thought about sitting down and having a nice long talk with her? She might open up to you."

"Oh Hunter, *please*. It's too late for that! She's been nothing but poison ever since she entered my life. She called me 'Stepchild' and nothing else our whole first year together. She moved my bed-room to the smallest tower and made me take my meals alone there. And she put all the candles on the floor."

Hunter looks at me. "What?"

"The candles. They're on the floor now, lining the rooms and the halls. At night, everyone is lit from below, which looks really creepy. And she keeps having my dresses made with bigger and bigger skirts."

Hunter's face fills with horror. "You think...."

I nod. "She was too afraid of my father to do something directly. But she loves to talk about how accidents can happen to children. Instead of wishing me goodnight, she says, 'Be careful, Snowy' – always with a smile. And then I climb the narrow stairs up to my little tower room. There's a candle sitting on every step and they are always burning."

Hunter slouches a little, exhaling. " I - I didn't know that."

I shrug. "It was nothing I couldn't handle. But then she took away my father.... You know, he wasn't the best of fathers, but he was *mine.* I won't let her go unpunished for this."

"But what can we do?" Hunter asks.

Smiling, I lift my hand and slide my fingers through his dense, dark hair. "When the time is right, we're going to steal her baby."

Chapter 3

We couldn't find a fairy. We did try – sort of. Hunter tied me to a tree and held his hunting knife against my throat while saying menacing things. But we were both struggling not to laugh. I guess fairies aren't so easily fooled.

The sun is setting as I return home and the castle glows warm and rosy as a peach. I sigh as I climb the rounded stairs, not wanting to go in. There is an unwholesome air about the castle these days, like a poisonous fog you can't see. But you feel it weighing down your heart.

Six months since I lost my father, King Edgar. The worst part is that I saw him just before he was murdered. I was watching from my tiny tower window.

He was far below, walking on the terrace with a beautiful lady. The lady was not Cinderella. As a child, I thought my father just had lots of friends that were ladies. As I grew older, I understood what it meant. He always took them to a tall, lonely tower that stood at the end of the terrace and they would go up alone. I have never been inside that tower. The door is always locked.

I watched my father enter with the beautiful lady. I saw the lights glowing behind the stained glass window of the room upstairs. A few minutes later, the window went dark. I waited for a long time but my father never came out. And neither did the beautiful lady.

In the morning, Cinderella sent the guards to search the tower. The door was still locked and they had to smash it in. They found nothing and no one at all. Then Cinderella went up and searched the tower herself. When she came out, she was smiling.

"Do you know where he is?" I asked.

"Gone," she said, the word a sigh.

"Gone *where?*" I asked.

Cinderella stroked my hair and spoke in her sweetest voice. "Most likely – to Hell."

My hands went cold, I felt sick all over. My poor father was dead. The beautiful lady – she must have been an assassin hired by Cinderella. I don't know what Cinderella found when she went up there, but the glee in her eyes was unmistakable. She looked triumphant.

That night, I cried myself to sleep. The next morning, I kicked every candle as I went down my staircase, watching them roll and crack into waxy chunks. Old Cinders had gone too far this time. I wouldn't kill her – that would be too kind.

And it's so much more satisfying to punish the living.

Chapter 4

I stand outside the double doors to Cinderella's chamber, my heart going high and fast. Even from here I can feel The Mirror. It's strong, which means Cinderella is standing before it. I know she will be there for hours.

I turn the handles and push through the doors. Cinderella's chamber was once luxurious, but now it's all become a shrine to The Mirror. Seriously. She banished all the furniture except for two iron candelabras that stick up like forks on either side of it. The rest of the room is bare as poverty. Cold as loneliness.

The Mirror is huge – floor to ceiling – and cut like an oval. The scrolling framework looks ancient, darkened by lack of care. No one ever cleans it and sticky cobwebs have stretched across the glass. It looks unbelievably heavy. And scary as death.

If Cinderella heard me enter, she doesn't turn. She stands before The Mirror in a lacy black dress that spills down and spreads out around her. Her golden hair is swooped up and swirled into a fancy coil. Her crown looks like some kind of silver claw that sticks up out of her head. She's a good Evil Queen, I'll give her that.

Cinderella's hands are pressed to The Mirror. Her head is tipped downward, the point of her crown touching the glass, and through the reflection I see her eyes, tightly shut. "Mirror, Mirror, on the wall...." She's panting, her voice growing hoarse. "Mirror...."

Something's wrong. She never looks like that. Usually, she stands proud and beautiful, mesmerized with her own reflection. Usually, she looks intoxicated with happiness.

"What's the matter?" I can't help asking. I'm still in the doorway and I won't come closer. Cinderella pushes off The Mirror's surface, face haggard, posture stooped.

"I don't know what I did," she says weakly. "It won't... I can't feel it."

"You can't feel The Mirror's presence?" That's odd, because I can feel it, thick as gravy. Lately, the feeling has grown stronger. I thought maybe The Mirror was gaining power, sucking life out of Cinderella. Or something like that.

Cinderella shakes her head, hugging herself. "It won't comfort me. It's like it doesn't know I'm here."

My eyes unintentionally rise to the glass and suddenly I feel it: the pull. Like a fishhook cast and sunk in my heart, it tugs me forward. The Mirror wants me to stand before it. And I find myself curious to hear what it has to say.

No! I take a hard step back and turn out to the hall where I can't see it. "Cinderella! Get OUT of there, it's making you sick!"

To my surprise, she slowly comes out. She looks like a sad little girl, all droopy. "I wonder why it doesn't want me," she murmurs.

"Forget that thing," I snap. "I want to talk to you, but not here. Can we go downstairs?"

She nods and we descend the long, curling staircase. Shortly after becoming queen, Cinderella had all the floors resurfaced in black marble and it was a massive project. But the sitting room she wanted completely white, everything from the curtains to the carpet. She said it was how *her* stepmother's sitting room had been. Considering she stabbed her own stepmother to death, I really don't know why she'd want that.

I ring for a servant to bring us tea. Cinderella stretches out on a chaise lounge, her belly a dark mound, the black dress shocking against the white velvet. After a few sips of tea, some redness returns to her cheeks.

"Ready to talk?" I don't actually feel sorry for her. There's no need to take pity on a cold-hearted killer.

Cinderella nods. Her eyes flick over me, up to my face. "You're looking very pretty today," she mutters.

I shrug. "So what?" *Why* does she always have to talk about that? Cinderella is gorgeous, she's got nothing to worry about. I wish she would try to think of something else.

"Anyway," I say, "tomorrow is my sixteenth birthday. Unfortunately, *my father* won't be here to celebrate it. But he always let me request a gift, one gift, whatever I wanted. And he always gave it."

"You're not a child anymore, Snowy," Cinderella says. "More importantly, you're not *my* child. Don't expect a gift from me."

Now I'm angry. That was really insensitive. "Look, all I want from you is an apple."

Cinderella looks at me. "An apple?"

"Yes. The Wood is thick with them now."

"Then go and pick one."

"I will. But I want you to do something to it."

"Do you fancy a pie for your birthday?"

"No. I want a Love Apple."

Cinderella draws back, surprised. "How do you know about that?"

"I looked through your book of spells. I know you've tried a few, down in the dungeon."

Cinderella shrugs. "A few. Some worked, some didn't. Magic is harder than I thought. And I cannot make you a Love Apple."

"Why not?"

"Because it's a light spell. Light Magic comes from love. Dark Magic comes from hate. That much I have learned. To make a Love Apple, I would need to feel love in my heart for someone. But I don't."

I narrow my eyes. "You love the baby."

Cinderella smiles and slides a hand over her bump. "I look forward to the baby. But that's not enough. Oh... did you find me a fairy?"

I roll my eyes. "Oh yes, she's waiting just outside the door."

Cinderella crooks an eyebrow at me. "Are you telling me that you failed?"

"Well no, I didn't fail because I didn't really try. Sorry, but life endangerment just isn't my thing."

Cinderella springs off the lounge and her hand swings high. I cringe, raising an arm to block the blow. But it doesn't come. After a moment, she drops her hand and folds back onto the lounge like a ribbon of silk. "All right. I'll do this the nice way." She clasps her hands together. "If you find me a fairy, I will make you a Love Apple. Is that fair?"

"You just said you can't make one."

"I can try. The memories of my father might stir a little love. Why is it you want this apple?" She smirks. "Is it because of that boy?"

I stiffen. "You know about him?"

"I have watched you with him through The Mirror. He seems sweet." Her smile is smeared with contempt.

She's been watching me and Hunter? Our enchanted moments together, when he holds my face and stares silently into my eyes.... When we have whispered conversations, our lips an inch apart, kissing lightly between the words.... Those moments belong to me, and to Hunter, and not to anyone else. I could kill her – *kill her!* – for violating that.

Now I have two ways to punish Cinderella. First I'm going to steal her baby. Then I'm going to smash The Mirror.

Chapter 5

Hunter offers me a small parcel, wrapped in brown cloth. He smiles. "Happy Birthday."

Grinning, I lay the parcel in my lap and unfold the wrappings. "Oh! Hunter, it's beautiful!" He has given me a dagger. A small dagger with a thin, steel blade and a handle studded with gem-stones. It comes with an ivory sheath and white belt so I can wear it over my dress.

Hunter smiles. "I think you should wear it whenever you're at home. If the queen is as dangerous as you say, you need some protection."

I sigh. We're sitting on our well, as usual, surrounded by the grove of glowing red apples. It feels so safe and serene here. I want it to be like this always, me and Hunter, side by side, our love a warm star that never stops shining. That's why I need the Love Apple. To keep him with me.

"Hunter, I'm tired of living under her cloud. I'm of age now, I can leave my home and she can't summon me back. We could find a place together, you and me, far away from here!"

"What about the baby?"

"We'll take the baby with us." To me it sounds perfect. Hunter and I living in a little cottage, raising the baby together. We would be like a family. A *happy* family, something I've never known.

Hunter slouches a little and kicks the heel of his boot against the well. I love how he dresses, so handsome and rugged. A white shirt, open at his throat, a brown leather vest, pants that show the thick muscles in his legs. "I don't feel right about taking the baby," he says. "It's hers."

"And my father was mine! But she had no scruples about taking him away from me. I have every right to take something from her, something just as precious."

"I don't think you miss your father."

"What?"

Hunter looks at me, his dark eyes troubled. "You have always seemed angry about it. Not sad. I think you just resent that Cinderella got away with it. You told me yourself that he always ignored you. And that he was cruel sometimes."

"He wasn't perfect. But he was still my father, the only family I had left. Even my grandparents are gone." My father's parents, King Stephen and Queen Shelley, had been lost soon after Cinderella joined our family. Their carriage slid off a mountain road. Wouldn't be surprised if Old Cinders was behind that too.

Hunter reaches around my shoulders and tugs me closer to him. "I'm sorry." He kisses the side of my forehead. "I just want you to be happy."

I take his free hand and bring it up to my cheek. "I am," I whisper, closing my eyes against the warmth of his palm. He guides my face up to his and we kiss softly and slowly, barely moving to feel the beauty of it. My heart hurts with love for him… and I like the hurt.

And then I wonder if Cinderella is watching us.

I pull away from Hunter, sighing.

"What's wrong?" he asks.

I shake my head. "Nothing." But I should have said "everything." How can we be free if Cinderella can see us? I will have to destroy The Mirror soon. But I'm afraid to think about it.

Hunter smiles and bumps his shoulder against me. "Come on, it's your birthday, let's have some fun. I'll let you try out my new crossbow."

"Really?" I hop onto the grass. Hunter lifts up a sturdy crossbow he had propped against the well. He bought it only a few days ago and said the arrows fly swifter and straighter than those of a long bow. Makes it easier for him to hunt large animals.

"Wait." I pick up my new dagger, slip it into its sheath, and fasten the white belt around my hips. The dagger hangs at my side, the gemstones like flashing bits of color over my white dress. "How do I look?" I tuck my arms behind my back.

Hunter grins. "Like an angel. But deadly."

He transfers the crossbow into my hands. "Oh, it's heavy!" I laugh as my arms sink beneath it. With a grunt, I hoist the bow higher.

"Try shooting an apple. No, not yet! Wait until I get behind you!" Hunter laughs, steps around me, and places his hand on my back. "Choose an apple, aim steady, and fire."

I pull the trigger and hear the snap and whistle of the arrow. Hunter and I wait in silence. "I don't think I killed an apple," I say.

"Try again," he says cheerfully. He takes the crossbow and loads another arrow into it.

"Maybe we can use this to find a fairy!" I cry. "I'll place an apple on my head and you can shoot it off me. That might make a fairy think I'm in danger." I know it sounds crazy but I really want the Love Apple.

Hunter looks horrified.

"I have faith in you," I say.

"And I'm flattered. But...." He takes my chin and looks at me in a way that paralyzes my body, holds me prisoner in his eyes. "I will not risk your life, my Snow Queen. Other than that, there is nothing I won't do for you."

I wink at him. "I will remember that."

Chapter 6

I feel happy as I walk home. Hunter and I have it all figured out. He's going to find a place for us. A cottage deep in The Wood. If he can't find one, he says he can build it. Don't know how he'll manage that, but it doesn't matter. I would live in a cave with Hunter.

For once, the palace doesn't feel foreboding as I enter. It's like the poisonous air evaporated and I feel welcomed and loved. Even the walls seem glad to see me.

And then I hear the screaming.

I was just about to go up to my room, but now I turn in the middle of the main corridor. It's far away but unmistakable. Long, trailing wails of agony, a grinding screech of rage and grief. My blood chills through at the sound of it.

I whirl around and race toward the screaming. There's only two things I can think of: either someone is actively torturing Cinderella, or she's about to have her baby.

I fly through the rooms and climb the curling staircase up to her chamber. The shrieks cut through my bones as I near the doors and I feel sickened with fear. Whatever is happening to her is truly horrific. I don't want to see, but I know I have to.

Two palace guards stand outside the doors, both of them pale. "What's *happening?*" I shout at them.

"We don't know," says the guard on the left. "She won't let us in, we were talking of breaking down the doors."

"CINDERELLA!" I push through the guards and bang my fist on the wood. "Cinderella, open up! What is happening to you?"

The screams cut off so suddenly I wonder if she died. But then I heard a shuffling, a scraping, rapid footsteps to the doors. I take a step back.

The doors snap open.

"It's YOOOU!" Cinderella screams. I've barely caught a glimpse of her wild eyes and fiery cheeks before she swings one of the iron candelabras at me. I gasp and dive sideways as the iron smashes the marble floor with a thunderous bang. "YOU!" She shrieks again, heaving the stick high.

"Cinderella!" I drop to the floor as she swings the iron again and it crashes through the window behind me, glass exploding. I scramble to the staircase on my knees and grab the railing.

"Get her, grab her, KILL HER!" Cinderella screams at the guards. But I guess they realize she's gone stark mad because they eye each other nervously and don't move.

I pull myself up and run down the stairs.

"Come BACK here, Stepchild!"

The iron candelabra hurtles past my head and hits the curling wall ahead of me. I gasp as it clangs down the marble steps, deafening as hammer blows. I shoot a frantic look over my shoulder. Cinderella is coming after me and now she's got a sword, probably one of the guard's. Her face is grimy-wet with tears and her hair is chaotic, loose shards hanging all over.

"STOP!" I cry out. I'm nearly at the bottom. I hear her grunt and something whistles past my shoulder, leaving a burning pain. Her crown – it cut me. She's throwing everything she's got on her.

I reach the floor but she's right at my heels. I drop again and hear the sword swish the air above my head. But she swung too hard and it flies from her hands, spinning across the floor of the parlor.

I try to stand up but she lunges and grabs the hem of my white dress.

"STOP IT! STOP!" I scream, frantically kicking my feet. She looks like a black spider crawling over me, especially with her bulging middle. "What is WRONG with you!"

"It doesn't *want* me anymore. It wants *you*." She says through her teeth. We're both writhing on the floor as she claws her way up my dress. "*You* are fairest! *You* are perfect! And today you're all... grown... up. So now it wants *you*."

I'm panting so hard my voice is in my breaths. My hands are tingling, painfully cold. She's got her weight on my chest, her face above mine. A red, sweating face with wet eyelashes and bared teeth. Eyes like flashing flames of blue.

"This is about the stupid MIRROR?" I shout.

"You can't... *have* it!" She snarls. "I will rip out your heart with my fingernails if I have to!"

Suddenly, I remember Hunter's gift. Reaching down, I yank the dagger out of its sheath, slashing it across her body. She gasps and pulls off me, her mouth opening wide. Her hand presses the underside of her chest.

I don't wait to see more. I spring up and dash across the parlor. I reach the main hallway and turn to the tall, double doors that lead out of the castle. She's screaming at me to come back but the sound is reassuring. She's not chasing me.

I pull on the heavy door and rush into the night. As I'm sprinting down the half-moon stairs, I notice little rivers of blood spilling down my right arm from the wound on my shoulder. My foot has just touched the gravel drive when I hear Cinderella's voice calling out from the parlor window.

"Do not think you can fly, little Snow! I will *find* you!"

Chapter 7

I keep running until I reach The Wood. I don't know if Cinderella will send the guards after me. Like the two idiots outside her chamber who did nothing to help me, thanks a lot, fellows! Too scared of the queen to make a move.

I slow down, winded, as the trees of The Wood close over me. It's too dark. If I keep running, I'll hurt myself. The moon slides blades of silver light through the trees but all else is blackness. I need to find the well... and Hunter.

My shoulder aches and I close my hand over it. It feels wet. I'm sure the blood has dripped on my dress by now. My white silk dress, iridescent in the moonlight.... I look around me. It's not good that I'm wearing white out here.

Oh, my heart. It won't stop battering. I can't believe Cinderella.... Well, I guess I can believe it, she always wanted to kill me. But the way she crawled over me with that wild rage in her eyes - oh, it was horrible! I'm going to have nightmares forever.

I walk carefully, lifting my knees with each step. My racing heart is keeping me warm but as soon as it quiets, I'll be cold. There's nothing on my arms and shoulders, except for a loose bit of sleeve. I need shelter. I need warmth. I need Hunter.

When I reach the well, he isn't there. And I'm dumb enough to be disappointed. Of course he's not here, he doesn't live at the well. I guess I hoped he would sense I'm in trouble and come to me.

I walk to the well, my arms hanging at my sides. I think the bleeding stopped. But what do I do? I don't know where Hunter lives. He told me he lives in one of the villages with his family but he's never taken me there. Hunter and I have always stayed in The Wood. It's where we felt safe.

I look at the grove of apple trees around me, tangled black knots in the darkness. I don't feel safe now. The Wood is not friendly at night, a place of harsh cries and crooked shadows, things that creep just beyond sight. Dangerous thieves are said to prowl The Wood at night, looking for unwary travelers. That would be me.

A chill wriggles up my spine and crinkles through my scalp. I'm starting to get cold. I rub my arms and look at the well but I don't want to sit there. There might be insects. I simply don't know what to do. I simply don't know where to go.

A branch cracks and I spin around. Two men step into the grove, abnormally large men. Both of them well over six feet, bearded and broad. They each carry a weapon that flashes the moonlight, axes or something. Though night darkens their faces, I can tell they're looking at me. I knew my white dress would call trouble.

"Lose your way, little miss?" one of them asks. His voice is neither friendly nor menacing, which scares me even more.

"No," I mumble, backing around the well. But as I do, I spot a third huge man further back in the forest, and then a fourth. My breaths jump in and out, sharp little gusts.

"Who are you?" I call out.

"We are known as The Dwarves," says the first man who spoke.

The Dwarves. Even I have heard of them, the most brutal gang of rogues in the kingdom. There's six or seven of them, so I've heard, all hulking, monstrous men. Few that have en-countered them survived to speak of it.

"Don't worry, little miss," says the first man. "Just leave us your coin purse and we'll let you walk free."

"I – I don't have a coin purse. Truly! I didn't bring one with me." My voice is squeaky-high and scared. I back away, holding up my shivering hands.

"Hmm...." The first man reaches up to stroke his beard. He doesn't sound angry. "Guess we'll be taking that pretty dress, then."

The man beside him gives a rough laugh. "And I get her after that!"

I turn and run with all my strength.

Chapter 8

I tear through the forest, my dress catching every branch and briar along the way. I hold up an arm to shield my face and feel the plants lash across my skin. Behind me, The Dwarves are crunching through underbrush, laughing as they pursue me. They don't sound the least bit worried I'll escape.

Then, far to my left, I see something. Small in the distance, but shining like the moon, I see a lady. A beautiful lady made of soft, golden light. She faces me with her hand outstretched, beckoning. Two delicate shapes fan out from her back and I realize this lady has wings....

A fairy!

Oh my stars, Old Cinders was right. I change course and sprint toward the fairy. She's come to help me in my peril, that's what they do, right? She'll get me away from The Dwarves.

I hear them calling out to each other; they've observed my change in direction. Instinctively, I know they cannot see the fairy. She's standing in a darker, denser part of The Wood, where the moonlight cannot find my dress. As I near her, I begin to see the features of her sweet face, the gauzy dress that drifts around her, the golden hair rippling over her shoulders-

And then she disappears.

I gasp as if struck. NO! Where did she go? The Dwarves are still chasing me, though the darkness confuses them, and I hear their frustrated curses. I sweep my eyes across the forest and with a surge of relief, I find her. She's off to the right, far ahead of me, and beckoning just like before. All right, I understand now. She's leading me somewhere.

I grab my skirt and raise it over my knees, gathering the bulk of the dress into a big, puffy bundle. I wrap my arms around it and run, my legs now free. The fairy stands silent and still as before, her hair and dress swaying gently. Again, just as I draw near, she vanishes. Moments later, she reappears like a twinkling star in the dis-tance. We go through the cycle several times.

I can't hear The Dwarves anymore, except for one faraway shout. They've lost my trail. My leg muscles burn but I continue to follow the fairy. I'm exhausted and shivering, damp with cold sweat. Wherever she's taking me, I sure hope it's warm.

The fairy stands before me, no more than a dozen yards ahead. She is so beautiful, a creature of light, with eyes kind as morning. I'm expecting her to disappear again but she raises an arm to her side. "Go through," she says in a hollow voice. And with the light emanating from her body, I see that she's brought me to the mouth of a cave.

And then she disappears.

The sudden darkness is sickening. I look around but she doesn't reemerge in the distance. The cave – this is my destination.

I creep inside, lightly touching my fingertips to the wall. The cave is low and the ceiling curves just above my head. I don't like this at all. Any-thing could be in here, bugs, bats, bears, you name it. And I won't see it coming.

The cave echoes my shaky breaths. I take one slow step at a time, my fingers trembling over the wall. The floor creeps upward as I go. Two tears slip out of me, warm on their release but cold when they reach my chin. Oh, this is horrible. This is so horrible.

Go *through*, the fairy said. Not go *in*. There must be something at the end, or on the other side. I sure hope the fairy was as good as she appeared and I'm not being lured into the jaws of a dragon.

My feet move upward, always upward, and the passage turns a few times. After some minutes, I feel a rush of cool air and sigh in desperate relief. *Air.* That means an opening. I'm going to come out of this worm hole.

The floor beneath me levels off and suddenly I see the exit. A mouth of pale light, as beautiful as dreaming. I grab my skirt and run toward it.

Cold air washes over me as I emerge from the cave. I drop my skirt and stand there, gaping at the land around me. I feel both scared and spellbound.

The moon is right above me, a lantern of peaceful light. I'm standing in a meadow, perfectly round, a circle cut from The Wood. The trees form a dark, jagged wall around the edge. Near the back of the meadow, a solitary tower looms above me, sharp and black against the sky. There's a door at the bottom, a window near the top, and a pointed roof covered in shingles. It's a very tall tower, at least five floors, and menacing as a spear.

With a hard sigh, I walk to the door, grass and leaves swishing beneath my feet. This was the worst, most terrifying day of my life. Happy Birthday, Snow White.

Chapter 9

I wake up stiff. There's no bed in this tower and I slept on the floorboards. In the darkness, I found a heavy piece of cloth and drew it over me for warmth. I was too tired to care how dirty it might be.

I shift up to my elbows and look around. I'm in a circular room, unpainted and unadorned. Looks like this used to be a guard tower. A rusted shield remains, some simple wood chairs, a broken spyglass. My makeshift blanket is actually a cape. To judge by the light, I'd say it's mid-morning.

I stand up, groaning. There's no mirror here – and just now mirrors are the *last* things I want – but I can tell I'm a mess. My arm is still smeared with my dried blood of yesterday and brown drops sprinkle the right side of my dress. My white skirt is dirty, torn in several places, and I think there are leaves in my hair.

I drift to the window and look out. I can see the palace from here, a few miles in the distance. This tower is tucked high in the hills, com-manding a long view of the kingdom. I can see why it would have been used by guards.

I cross the room and head down the staircase which curls along the wall. The room below looks like it was used for eating, the room below that, for sleeping. There are five rooms in all, one above the other.

When I step outside, the dark memories of last night fade away. This spot is beautiful, the trees burning with autumn colors, the tower weathered and mossy. I smile as I step back to look at it. Hunter and I could live here. We would make it our own, paint every room, plant little gardens. And be together.

I'm not thrilled about having to go through the cave again, but it's not so bad the second time. At least I know now where it takes me.

I step cautiously back into The Wood, my eyes alert for Dwarves. I see nothing but sunlight and shrubbery, hear nothing but chattering birdcalls. I hope I can find my way back to the well without getting lost. I need to talk to Hunter.

I've gone about half the distance when I hear someone say, "Snowy?"

I whirl around, my mind full of Dwarves. But it's only Hunter, carrying his crossbow. "Hunter!" I cry out, running to him with open arms. I see him noticing my odd appearance, his dark brows drawing together. He catches me when I throw myself against him and cradles me gently.

"Hunter, Hunter, Hunter," I sob into his neck.

"What happened to you?" he asks.

"So much! We need to talk."

"Sure." Tucking me under his arm, he walks me through the forest until we find a fallen tree. He holds both my hands as we sit down. "You're hurt," he says, touching my shoulder.

"Cinderella did it." I tell Hunter everything that happened. Unfortunately, this means I have to talk about The Mirror. He looks bewildered at first, then more and more disturbed as I go on.

"What does it do?" he asks.

I open my hands. "It... changes how you feel about yourself. If it likes you, that's good. If it doesn't like you... it's awful."

Once, two years ago, Cinderella brought me in front of The Mirror. Honestly, I think she wanted to see what would happen. Out of curiosity, I co-operated. I felt The Mirror's aura settle over me, wrapping me like a thick shawl. I looked at my reflection and I couldn't look away.

My reflection was distorted but I didn't know it. I saw myself as The Mirror saw me, small, ugly, useless. My limbs were thin as starvation, my face skeletal, my eyes sunken and dark. My utter worthlessness sank through me, heavy as a broken heart. No one as hideous as I was de-served to go on living. With one wordless thought, I begged The Mirror to end my wretched life. It released the aura so I could move.

I headed to the window and climbed on the sill, calm as sleepwalking. Cinderella simply watched me. Then my father came into the room, shouted at Cinderella, and pulled me off the sill. He carried me downstairs while I whimpered and shivered and tried to keep him from seeing my face. It took me three days to realize I was not the creature I'd seen in The Mirror.

Chapter 10

Next I tell Hunter about the Dwarves. His face changes here, mouth hardening into a line. It is rare that I ever see Hunter look angry.

"Do not worry," he says in a firm voice. "They won't trouble you again."

"Why?" I say. "Can you stop them?" Not that I don't believe in Hunter, but those guys were monsters.

"Just don't worry. I'll take care of it."

I look at him. "The first person we need to take care of is Cinderella. She's lost her mind, Hunter. If we don't do something, she will hunt me down and kill me."

"But what can we do?"

I look down at the crossbow which Hunter propped against the fallen tree, then back up at his face. "We can hunt her first."

Hunter blinks. "What?"

"We will never be safe, so long as she lives. She always wanted to kill me off. And now she thinks her demon mirror prefers me to her. She'll do *anything* to make The Mirror take her back. That's why we have to kill her first." I rest my hand on his knee and speak in a whisper. "*You* have to do it."

Hunter flinches. "I can't."

"It's not murder," I say soothingly. "You'd be defending me, saving my life. Like a hero! Did you not say you would do anything for me?"

He shakes his head. "Please don't ask it of me."

"You didn't see her, Hunter. She said she would rip out my heart with her fingers. If you don't do this for me, I'm as good as dead! Do you want that?"

"No, but... killing her will also kill the baby."

I forgot about that. I think for a moment. "Aim high. The baby will be fine. Once Cinderella is dead, we can get it out of her."

Hunter leans back, horrified.

I exhale impatiently. "Haven't you ever gutted a deer? I know you have, this is no different. You are a hunter, Hunter. *Hunt* her!"

Hunter looks away from me. I feel bad at how conflicted he looks; the poor boy is too sensitive. I will have to be brave for both of us.

"I think the queen is misunderstood," he says. "Can't we just destroy The Mirror?"

"Yes, we can. But Cinderella goes first, I'm not backing down on that. If you love me as you say, you will protect me. Do you love me, Hunter?"

Hunter's leaning on his knees, his head bowed. His rakes his fingers through his thick, dark hair. Then, with his eyes closed, he gently nods his head.

Chapter II

Hunter and I make our plans to kill the queen. We will meet at the well at sundown. Hunter is going to bring me some clothes, something more practical than my poufy white gown. I have to show him the entrance to the secret passage that leads inside the castle. From there he will go on alone. The guards, I suspect, will be under orders to kill me on sight. I will return to the tower and wait for Hunter there.

I'm thrilled to learn Hunter didn't know about the tower. He has seen the cave but never went in, since caves are not considered safe places to explore. That means our tower is well hidden. I tell Hunter about my plans to turn it into a home for us, but he doesn't seem to be listening. I can tell he's nervous about what he has to do.

He presses me against him before he leaves; kisses me between my eyebrows. He lends me a hunting knife from his belt, since I dropped my pretty dagger when I attacked Cinderella. Once he's gone, I head back to the tower, noting landmarks along the way. I need to memorize how to find this place.

I grab apples off the trees and eat them as I go. Oh my stars, I'm so hungry. I think about the Love Apple. Cinderella won't make it for me now, which worries me. I need that apple for me and Hunter.

A Love Apple, according to the spell book, will grant everlasting happiness to you and your lover. It will keep your love as fresh and magical as when it first blossomed, never letting your hearts grow weary, like those of an old married couple. And it prevents your lover from ever straying to someone else. Both of you must bite the apple to complete the spell. And then you live happily ever after.

I grope my way through the cave again and return to the meadow with the tower. My heart is much lighter now. Soon I'll be rid of Old Cinders and the darkness she brought into my life. I explore the clearing for a while and discover some raspberry bushes at the edge of the forest, and a bit further back, a shallow stream. I cup my hands and drink the cold water, then wash the dry blood off my arm. I will try to clean up the tower next, though it won't be easy without a broom. I need to make things suitable for the baby.

I can't help smiling as I think about it. That baby is the only thing Cinderella cares about. And I'm going to take it from her. So in a way, I'm doing to her what *she* wanted to do to me. I am ripping out her heart.

Chapter 12

Hunter, always early, is waiting for me when I return to the well. He's got a leather pack slung over his shoulder and from it he draws a simple gray dress. "It was my mother's. But I think it will fit you."

"Thank you!" I take the dress and slip behind the broad trunk of an oak, to change. It's a much more sensible dress than the white – at least the skirt isn't three feet wide. I feel as cute as a little peasant maiden.

When I return, Hunter is holding his elbows and frowning. "I've thought of a problem. If we kill the queen, who will rule the kingdom? You'll have to do it, you're next in line. Which means we can't live in that tower."

"I don't want to rule the kingdom," I say firmly. "It never makes anyone happy. Let the people find a new ruler among themselves."

"It will throw our land into chaos."

"Oh Hunter, now you're stalling. None of this changes the fact that we *have* to kill Cinderella, or she will kill me. The rest will sort itself out."

Hunter sighs. I give him a comforting hug and rub his back. I wish I could go with him, to help him be brave. But it's far too dangerous.

"So where is this secret passage?" he asks.

I point to the well behind us. "Right here."

Hunter stares at me in disbelief.

I giggle. "It is! It starts in the dungeons below the castle and ends here at the well. It was built as an escape route for the royal family in case they were under attack. But those who know how can also use it to get *into* the castle." I beckon him to the side of the well that has crumbled down. We crouch on the dirt and peer inside. Much of the well's inner shaft is grown over with ivy, so it's hard to see far. "Look there." I point to the far side of the shaft. "There's an iron rung built into the wall, like the step of a ladder. Do you see it?"

Hunter nods.

"There are more of them. You can climb down. Now, once you're at the bottom, it'll be tricky. There's a tiny door, about half your height, made to look like the wall. You'll have to crouch and push until it opens for you. From there the passage leads straight to the castle."

"And what do I do about the guards?"

I hesitate. I know what *I'd* do if I had a crossbow and came face-to-face with those cowards who did nothing to help me yesterday. But I'm made of tougher stuff than Hunter.

"Avoid them if you can," I say. "Take the back stairs used by the servants until you get to the main floor. If you get caught, say you've been summoned by the queen to hunt the traitor, Snow White. They might take you to her."

Hunter nods without looking at me. He secures the crossbow to his back, shifts his legs into the well, and lowers himself in. When only his head and shoulders are still above ground, he turns to me, one hand gripping the top rung of the iron ladder. "Wish me luck," he says with an uneasy smile.

I'm still crouched on my knees, so I lean forward and kiss him, my hands holding both sides of his face. For the first time ever, I feel reluctance from him, like he's only receiving the kiss and not giving it. I will have to get the Love Apple soon.

I draw back but let my lips hover just above his. "Kill her quickly," I whisper. "And bring me the baby. I'll be waiting for you at the tower."

"I will come," he says. And then he drops out of sight, into the well.

Chapter 13

Back at the tower, I find a shallow wood crate with some walnuts at the bottom. I shake them out, carry the crate up to the high room, and stuff it with my white dress. There. Now the baby has a soft place to sleep.

There's still a lot that we will need. Tables and chairs and pots and bowls and curtains and rugs. And a bed for me and Hunter. My body blushes hot at the thought of it. I will need to find a friar to marry us first. Hunter is the noble sort and I know he won't share the bed with me until he's made me his wife.

I walk to the window, though night has settled in and I can't distinguish the trees from the sky. It should be over now. Hunter should have the baby in his arms, heading back to me through The Wood. And Cinderella should be dead in the palace, lying in a lake of her own blood. I hope he did it in front of The Mirror.

My stomach grumbles so I eat a handful of raspberries I collected earlier. I wonder if the baby is a boy or a girl. I will have to choose a name for this infant who will be both my child and my sibling. I doubt we'll look alike, though. Cinderella and my father were both blonde, but I have the midnight hair and eyes of my mother.

I remember my own mother well. She died when I was six due to some trouble with her lungs, my father said. She was as beautiful as sculpted ice, with haunting eyes that seemed to harbor a dark secret. She told me that my beauty came from her, but also from magic. Blood Magic, she called it. She said she would explain it to me when I was older. But, of course, that day never came. I miss my mother. If she hadn't died, Old Cinders would never have come. I would still have my family.

I'm now feeling nicks of impatience. Hunter should have returned by now. I strain my ears at the window, hoping to hear crackling footsteps or the feeble cry of an infant. Perhaps things did not go as planned. I should have gone with him, but I was afraid of Cinderella, and the palace guards, and more than anything else - The Mirror.

Although I didn't tell Hunter this, I know Cinderella was right: The Mirror wants me now. I have felt it for weeks, I just didn't understand. I won't let it find me. I won't let it control me.

I hope he made it past the guards. I hope he killed Cinderella but not the baby. I hope he was strong enough to cut the baby from her. I hope he got out of the palace. I hope he wasn't attacked by Dwarves in the forest. I hope he will be here soon.

All night long, I hope and I hope. But my Hunter does not come.

Chapter 14

I walk through The Wood at a hard, steady pace. Hunter never came back. Once morning gave me enough light to see by, I set out with the hunting knife clutched in my hand. He must have been caught, imprisoned at the palace. Well, I'll get him out. Even if I have to slay every guard in my path.

The forest is a sleepy gray, the sky wearing a wooly blanket of clouds. I'm still far from the palace, moving around clusters of oak and chestnut trees. It's dim even in daylight and too leafy to see far ahead. Someone should really cut a path through this place, it would make getting through a lot easier.

And then a Dwarf steps right in front of me.

I stop in pure shock. I don't think he knew I was coming either, because his bushy eyebrows shoot up. He's holding a wooden club with iron spikes at the end. The thing is nearly as tall as I am.

He gives a short nod. "Morning, miss. Glad I ran into you." He looks beyond me and raises his voice. "Hey, fellows, look who's here!"

Oh NO! I whirl around but more Dwarves are creeping out behind me, pushing through ferns and around trees. They're all enormous, close to seven feet. Oh my stars, I'm a dead girl.

I spin back to face the one in front of me. I jab my arm upward and point the hunting knife at his face. A ripple of rough laughter circles around me.

The Dwarf ahead of me smiles. He's got sandy hair and a short beard, both untidy. One of his eyebrows has been split at the center by a deep scar. But despite all that, there's something familiar about him.

"Put it down, little miss, won't do you no good. Sorry we scared you the other night, we didn't know you were Hunter's gal."

I drop my arm in surprise. "What?"

"We don't harm each other's women. It's in the code, more or less. Keeps us all on friendly terms that way."

"Us?" I ask, bewildered.

"Us!" The Dwarf laughs and lifts his arms, gesturing to the six other men. "And our brother Hunter too, of course."

I keep perfectly still. I can't process what I'm hearing. "Hunter is... your brother?"

"We're all brothers," the Dwarf says. "Hunter's the youngest."

"Hunter is a *Dwarf!*"

The seven men all rumble with laughter.

"Naw, he's too small for that," the Dwarf says. "He came from Pa's second wife, so he didn't get the big bones of our mother. She was solid."

"So Hunter is your half-brother."

"Brother is brother!" the Dwarf says gruffly. "What, he didn't tell you about us?"

I shake my head. All Hunter ever said was that he lived with his family. Oh boy, are *we* going to have a long talk!

"Probably didn't want to push his luck. Really bowled us over when he said he was courting the princess. He was none too happy we chased you the other night."

"Yeah, sorry about that," says another Dwarf with a dark, longer beard. They all look at least thirty or older, but even with their lined faces and hard scowls, I can see traces of Hunter. His father must have married again late in life.

I shake my head. "It's... it's...." No, I can't say it's all right. They did scare me out of my wits. "It's time for me to go. You won't stop me?"

"Nope!" The Dwarf steps aside, raising a hand to the forest ahead of me. I manage a smile as I pass him. "And what do I call you if we should meet again?"

"Cooper." He claps a huge hand on my shoulder. "I'm glad Hunter found you, you're a right pretty wench. But just so you know, if you ever hurt him, we'll split you open and eat your heart and liver for supper." He smiles pleasantly.

I crook an eyebrow at him. "And my spleen for dessert?"

That gets a thunderous roar from all the men. Cooper slaps my back, still laughing. "On your way, Princess."

"Call me Snowy." I've gone about three steps more when a sudden thought strikes. I turn back. "What if someone *else* was hurting Hunter? Like the queen, for example. What would you do then?"

Cooper's eyebrows drop low. "Why do you ask?"

"I think you all had better come with me to the palace."

Chapter 15

On the way, I tell Cooper how the queen tried to kill me. I say that Hunter offered to go "talk" to her about it – that's all they need to know. But I think the queen locked him up, instead.

The other Dwarves follow in silence. They all, basically, look like each other, just with varying shades of brownish hair and beards of different lengths. Their arms and exposed bits of chest are hairy. I'm *so* glad Hunter did not inherit those traits.

We approach the palace steps and I have to admit I feel powerful. I've got seven scary men behind me, all armed with deadly weapons. The palace guards have almost never been challenged. They will drop like flies before us.

"I want Cooper to stay with me," I say. "The rest of you make it your mission to find Hunter. Strike down anyone that tries to stop you. He is probably down in the dungeon."

"What are we going to do?" Cooper asks.

"*We* are going to look for the queen." If Hunter was unable to finish his task, then I must finish it for him. Cooper will help. I can tell he likes me; we've struck some kind of chord. We're both bad apples, but lovable.

We climb the round staircase. At the top, two guards stand beside the double doors. They look, to say the least, surprised to see me. Even more surprised to see my cohort of thugs.

"Open the doors," I say smoothly. "And don't make me ask twice."

The guards obey without a squeak of protest. The Dwarves and I march into the main corridor of the castle. It lies before us like a black ribbon, the marble floor gleaming. Doors and chandeliers appear again in the floor, as if frozen under a dark lake.

"Find him. Search every room if you have to," I say to the Dwarves. "Cooper, come with me."

First I check Cinderella's white sitting room. She isn't there. Then I lead Cooper to the parlor where she attacked me. I find my jeweled dagger on the floor and slip it back into my belt. Ahead of us is the long staircase that curls up to Cinderella's chamber. And I can feel The Mirror. It knows I'm here.

"Go on up," I say to Cooper. "I'll stay here and keep watch. The queen is probably in her chamber. If the door is locked, break it open. You'll see a large mirror on the wall. Make *sure* you don't look directly at it. And bring the queen down to me."

"Why, what for?" Cooper asks.

"We will make her tell us where Hunter is." And once that's over, I will *end* the reign of the Evil Queen.

Cooper heads up the staircase, stepping over the iron candelabra that still lies across the lower steps. His face is grim and he holds the spiked club at a ready angle. I almost feel sorry for Cinderella.

I back against the nearest wall, feeling the need for something solid behind me. I hear bangs and echoed shouts through the walls as the other Dwarves search the palace. The running feet of palace guards, the screams of frightened servant maids. And I can't help smiling. This dreary castle could use some chaos.

Cooper clomps down the stairs. "Nobody's up there."

"No?" I'm surprised. "Well... maybe she's in the throne room."

But the throne room is barren as a graveyard. The crystal chair sticks up like a headstone at the top of the room. I sit down, always stunned at its unyielding firmness, and tap my fingers against the arm. "Where could she be...."

The six other Dwarves tromp into the room, panting like they've run through the whole palace. "No Hunter," says one of them. "We tried every room, the dungeons too. He's not here."

Cooper frowns. He hoists up his club until it's level with my face. "If this is some kind of trick, little miss-"

"It's not. It's not." I hold up a hand, thinking hard. Honestly, I'm too worried to even listen to his threats. "No, he definitely came here to see the queen. But now they're both gone." I can't figure it out. Cinderella is a small woman, about to give birth. What could she possibly do to Hunter?

"Bring in the guards," I say. "Maybe they saw what happened."

One of the Dwarves makes a snorting sound. "You'll have to wait until they're conscious again."

I curse and that makes the Dwarves laugh. But I'm in no mood. I need to find out what happened to Hunter. And not just because the Dwarves might kill me if I don't. I'm scared for him. He is my Hunter. I wish I could *see* what happened when he came here.

I close my eyes. "Oh, no...."

"What?" Cooper says.

I grip the arms of the throne. There has to be another way.... But no, I know there isn't. It scares the blood out of me. But I can do it for Hunter. He would do it for me.

"Um... are you fellows hungry?" I look past Cooper to the other Dwarves. "Why don't you go to the kitchen while Cooper and I figure this out? Help yourselves to whatever is there. Just... don't hurt the cook, all right?"

"Sounds good to me," says the Dwarf with the dark beard. The six of them leave the throne room, lightly swinging their weapons. I slide out of the chair and already feel sick to my stomach.

"What's your plan?" Cooper says.

"There's only one way to find out what happened to Hunter," I say softly. "I have to ask The Mirror."

Chapter 16

I climb the curling staircase to Cinderella's chamber with Cooper behind me. I gave him a quick explanation about The Mirror, said it had magical powers but could also be dangerous. He looks skeptical, to put it mildly, but he doesn't argue with me.

One of the doors stands ajar from when Cooper searched the room. I can't see The Mirror, but I can feel it reaching for me, coaxing me to come in with long, curling fingers.

"Can you feel it?" I whisper to Cooper.

"Feel what?" he says.

"Never mind. The last time I looked in The Mirror I nearly killed myself. I want you stand in front of the window and stop me if that happens again. In fact, if I do *anything* strange, drag me out of the room."

Cooper frowns. "Maybe this isn't a good idea."

"It isn't. But it's the only way to find Hunter."

I touch the handle and slowly push the door open, keeping my eyes on the floor. Cooper goes and stands by the window, like I asked. I turn, shut the door, and draw a deep breath. Oh, I'm so scared.

I turn back to the room, my eyes still lowered. Though I'm not looking directly at it, I can see it. Huge and dark and ovular, like a great mouth waiting to swallow me. I wrap my arms around my body, over the simple grey dress Hunter gave me. With awkward, shuffling footsteps, I creep toward The Mirror.

It's glad to see me. Waves of love and warmth wash over me and I almost feel as if I'm being caressed by ghostly hands. But I resist. I don't want to feel happy. I just want to know where Hunter is.

I'm now standing in front of it. Still hugging my sides, my head downward, my hair a black waterfall around my face. Cinderella used to talk to The Mirror, out loud. I don't want to – it feels stupid – but I guess I have to try.

"C-can you tell me where Hunter is, please?"

I feel another wave of warmth and a message comes with it. *Look.*

No, I don't want to look. I just want an answer.

The Mirror is waiting. Patiently. Lovingly. All it wants me to do is look. It won't hurt me. It won't frighten me.

I'm shaking with the fight to resist. Looking gives it power, I have seen that with Cinderella. But if I don't look, it won't tell me. And I have to find my Hunter.

Slowly, I turn up my face and I lift my eyes.

There's a girl in the mirror. A young girl, no more than eight years of age. She is small and soft and gentle. Everything about her is beautiful, her delicate hands, her shining black hair, her tiny pink mouth that smiles sweetly. I can feel this child is precious, so precious to The Mirror. And the child is me.

Like a well flooding over, emotion surges through my body and my eyes fill up and drop tears. I have not felt like anyone's precious child since I lost my mother. I felt abandoned. Often, I still feel like a child that needs someone's arms to curl into. I wasn't expecting this, that The Mirror would understand me. That it would know me.

I'm no longer afraid. I feel calm and confident. I know how to speak to The Mirror.

"Mirror, Mirror, on the wall. Where is my Hunter, brave and tall?"

Chapter 17

My reflection fades. A scene appears before me as if I'm looking through a window. I see the dungeon and a stone slab on the floor shifting sideways. Hunter climbs out, emerging from the secret passage. The Mirror makes me understand that what I'm looking at has already taken place.

He creeps through the dungeon, his eyes alert and wary. Slowly, he makes his way up through the palace, easily avoiding the idiot guards who have grown too used to safety. I gave Hunter instructions on how to reach Cinderella's chamber. After a few wrong doors, he locates the parlor and the stairs that lead up to her room.

I feel proud as I watch him. He's as silent as a bobcat, his face expressionless. As he glides up the stairs, he slowly eases the crossbow off his back. My heart begins to pound with excitement. Maybe he did it. Maybe the reason I haven't seen him is because he's out burying her body.

Hunter reaches the top of the stairs and the corridor that runs outside Cinderella's chamber. The angle shifts so I can see what he sees. The doors to Cinderella's chamber are closed. And she's lying on the floor outside of them.

I mean it. Cinderella is lying on the floor, in her long black dress, shut out of the room that holds her precious mirror. She's curled up like a sleeping cat, her back facing Hunter. Talk about the perfect target.

Hunter crouches on one knee and lifts the crossbow. For a long minute, he simply stares at her, his finger hovering over the trigger.

Come on, Hunter, I think. *Just do it!*

Cinderella stretches and rolls onto her back. She sees Hunter. Slowly, she pushes herself up until she's sitting against the door. Her hand is pressed to the place where I cut her, above the swell of her stomach. I don't know why Hunter doesn't shoot her now. Her face looks dead already.

Her beautiful blue eyes gaze at Hunter. Not afraid. Not surprised. "Go on," she says in a lifeless voice. "It's the kindest thing you can do for me."

Hunter's crossbow lowers. And with it, my heart.

"Why are you sad?" he asks in that tender voice that could conquer a kingdom.

Cinderella is quiet for a long time. Then she says, "Everyone... leaves me. No matter how much I need them. Papa.... Godnutter.... The Mirror. I am always... left alone."

"You're not alone," Hunter says softly. "But I do think you're ill. When did you eat last?"

Cinderella closes her eyes. "It doesn't matter."

"All right." Hunter slings his crossbow over his back and smiles at her. "If nothing matters, then you won't mind coming with me. I'm taking you away from this place."

"No...." Cinderella moans. But she doesn't fight when Hunter hoists her to her feet. He guides her down the stairs, his arm around her shoulders, and when a palace guard appears, he says he's taking her out for some air. Since Cinderella appears to be cooperating, the guard lets them go.

I watch Hunter lead her out of the palace. Then the scene disappears and I'm staring at the ordinary reflection of my face.

"No. NO!" I smack the glass with my palm. "I'm not done yet, where did he take her?"

The glass doesn't change. But the word *Safe* enters my mind.

"What happened?" Cooper asks gruffly.

I turn to him, annoyed. The Mirror's aura is gone and I feel cold without it. "Hunter is fine. He found the queen sick and wounded and he took her away. Someplace safe. That's all it will tell me."

"Safe?" Cooper looks like he's thinking about it. "Probably our cottage, can't think where else he'd go."

"Your cottage?"

"Aye, most likely. I'll have one of the fellows go check. Barker can do it."

I nod. "Tell him to bring Hunter back, if he's there. But not the queen. Tell him to remind Hunter that he must finish his task."

"What task?"

"He'll know."

Cooper shrugs. "If you say so, miss. I'll talk to Barker." He leaves the room and I hear his heavy tread on the stairs.

I sneak a tentative glance at The Mirror. And suddenly I'm struck by how ugly this little gray dress is. A princess shouldn't look like that. I will go up to my room and change immediately.

Chapter 18

It is nightfall when Barker returns. I wait for him in the crystal chair. I'm now wearing a white dress with long, tight sleeves and a full skirt embroidered with intricate silver swirls. I feel much better.

"Well?" I ask. "Where is Hunter?"

Barker bows before me. He looks older than Cooper, with gray hairs mixed into his long, dark beard. He usually carries a huge battle axe and his left hand is missing two fingers.

"He's at our cottage. The queen's there too. He wants to speak with you at the well tomorrow, the usual time, he says."

I narrow my eyes. "He wouldn't come back with you?"

"He said he wants to talk to you first. He said not to worry."

"Did you see the queen?"

"No. Hunter said she was resting."

Oh, I do not like this at *all*. Hunter and Cinderella alone in a cottage. I don't care if she's sick and pregnant, that woman if full of wicked wiles. I've seen the effect her beauty has on men. They can't even move when they see her.

I rise from the throne and look at Cooper. He's standing behind Barker with the other Dwarves. "Take me to this cottage," I say.

Cooper chuckles. "What's your hurry? It's dark and it's cold and it's far. You can wait for tomorrow."

"No, I cannot. You will take me there now."

Cooper smirks. "That's not what Hunter wants, little miss. Don't you *care* about what he wants?" His voice carries a hint of menace.

I stamp my foot. Look at them, seven brutes all towering above me. Any one of them could snap me in half. This isn't fair, I have no power.

"Fine!" I snap. "But if I'm staying, you all have to stay here with me. I need protection. You can have the whole palace, eat what you want, take what you want, I don't care. So long as you stay."

"Fair enough," Cooper says. "Beats prowling through The Wood in the dark, hunting strangers for a few coins. We'll look after you – for now."

"Thank you," I say coldly. "Now if you'll excuse me, I'm very tired. I barely slept last night. Help yourselves to whatever bedrooms you want, there are plenty." I spring off the chair and sweep out of the throne room, hoping I look haughty.

Guess I don't have to sleep in my little tower room now that Cinderella is gone. Oh, who cares, I'm used to it. I'm heading down the hall, looking forward to my bed, when suddenly I feel it: the tug in my chest. The Mirror wants me.

I stop while I think about it. Darn, I want to go. I want to see if The Mirror approves of my dress, I could tell it didn't like the last one. I wonder if I'll look like a little girl again, or if my appearance will change each time....

NO! I said I wouldn't do this. I won't let The Mirror control me. But the pull is so strong. I feel hurt because Hunter wouldn't come to me. And frustrated with the Dwarves. At least The Mirror would be a distraction. Maybe it would comfort me, make me feel wonderful again.

I turn around. Five minutes. That's all.

Chapter 19

This time, I'm the one who arrives early at the well. I'm burning with impatience to see Hunter. I wear the same white-and-silver dress as yesterday, plus a delicate tiara in my hair. Hunter needs to see that I'm prettier than Cinderella.

He comes! My heart leaps to the sky when he steps into the grove. He grins at me and holds out his arms. I rush into them and squeeze him tight, even though part of me wants to smack him.

"Hunter, you scared me to death!"

"I'm sorry, Snowy." He rubs my back and kisses the top of my head. "I just couldn't do it. She looked so sad. I thought if I got her away from that mirror thing, she might get better. We won't have to kill her."

"Hunter, you don't know her. Believe me, she is pure evil. Soon as she's well, she'll come after me."

I push back and give him a dry look. "By the way, I met your brothers."

Hunter laughs. "I'm so sorry! I should've told you, but.... I was afraid of scaring you away." His face becomes serious. "Are they treating you well?"

"They're fine. They're at the palace with me. I can't *believe* you're related to them! I heard the Dwarves kill and eat every person they rob!"

"The eating part isn't true. But they're brutes, no question. They rob for the fun of it, it's easier than working. I can't stop them, no one can. But they're loyal to family. So long as they think you're with me, they won't bother you."

"You need to come back with me to the palace."

Hunter sighs. "I will, but... not yet, Snowy."

I fold my arms.

"Just give me some time," he says. "I want to help the queen; I think it will solve our problems."

"That wasn't the plan. You could kill her easily now. And take the baby. And we'll go to the tower. *That* was the plan."

"But...." Hunter reaches out and takes hold of my fingers. "Isn't it better to spare a life if there's hope for that person? I don't think she's as bad as you say."

"What has she been doing?"

"Sleeping, mostly. I got her to eat a little. She just needs someone to look after her."

"Fine! You come back to the palace with me. We'll send one of your brothers to look after her."

"We can't do that and you know it. My brothers are savages. If she made them angry they would beat her to death."

"That's good!"

"Snowy." Hunter looks right in my eyes. "I can't come back with you today. I'm asking you to understand. Can you do this for me?"

No, I cannot. Cinderella took away my father. She does *not* get to take away my Hunter. I set my jaw. "Where is this cottage?"

Hunter's face closes off. "I can't tell you."

I stamp my foot. "This isn't fair! All I want is for us to be together!"

"And I want that too. We'll get there. When the queen is well, we'll send her back to the palace. Then you and I will go far away and live in peace. We don't need her baby, Snowy. We can have one of our own."

"So now you make all the decisions?"

"I just want to make everyone happy. Please do me a service when you return to the palace. Tell one of my brothers to destroy that mirror."

I flinch. "Why?"

"The queen whimpers about it in her sleep. I don't understand it, but it's dangerous. It needs to be removed from her life. You haven't gone near it, have you?"

"No," I say, feeling guilty because it's a lie. But some things not even Hunter can understand. "I'll take care of it."

He smiles. "Thank you, Snowy." He pulls me in and kisses me slowly, his mouth gently pinching my top lip and then the bottom. His hand slides into my hair and curls around the back of my neck. My heart flutters like a hummingbird's wings. Oh my Hunter! I never want to let him go.

He releases me, smiling. "Meet me here again tomorrow. And don't worry. We'll be fine."

I grin. "I will come."

The glow from his kiss lasts until I'm back at the palace. I barely notice the Dwarves have raided the armory and are trying out the weapons on each other, making the throne room sound like a battlefield. I'm so, so happy. And now I know what to do.

Poor Hunter. Sweet Hunter. He thinks he can redeem the queen. But I know better. She has to die and I must do it myself.

I'll just have to be sneaky about it.

Chapter 20

The Dwarves and I have a fabulous supper. One of them – I don't know all their names yet – can cook. Which is good because I found out most of the servants have taken off in pure fear. Anyway, the Dwarf who cooks made a huge meal that consisted mostly of meat: legs of mutton, sides of ham, two fat geese, huge venison steaks. I join them for supper but oh my stars, they eat like barbarians. Ripping the meat with their fingers, laughing through mouths full of food, hurling the bones over their shoulders. I'm shocked at first, but then I start tearing into the food like they do. It's fun!

Afterwards, I creep upstairs to see The Mirror. I need to ask it a few things. I still get nervous whenever I'm near it, but it's not so bad now. I no longer think it will hurt me.

Last night, I carried back upstairs the iron candelabra that Cinderella used to assault me. Now I light them on both sides of The Mirror. They create a hazy glow that pulses like a fearful heart and puts quivering shadows behind me. My eyes circle to the top of the golden frame where cobwebs float across the curling metal. I see a black spider crawling over the top, its hooked legs silently groping. And I shudder. The Mirror still creeps me out.

What is this thing? Where did it come from? Why does it seem to be *alive*, have thoughts and feelings like a person? The Mirror has been here all of my life, long before Cinderella ever came. I remember my mother brushing her hair in front of it. But it didn't seem weird then; I never felt a presence. And my mother never talked to it. I guess I shouldn't trust something I don't under-stand, but magical things are always a mystery, right?

I give the glass a careful smile. "Mirror, Mirror, on the wall. Who is fairest of them all?"

At first, my reflection looks like me. Then it changes. I look like a queen, the most breath-taking queen imaginable. My skin is pale and perfect as moonlight. My hair shines like spilled ink. The Mirror has given me a crown made of glass, and a dress that glistens like a field of new snow. A queen as harsh and beautiful as winter. That's how it sees me.

I feel exquisitely happy. I understand now why Cinderella always asked The Mirror who was fairest. I thought it was just an obsession with her appearance, but it means so much more. The one who is fairest is the one most loved. When we love someone, that person becomes more beautiful than any other creature. And now *I* am fairest. Beautiful and beloved.

I close my eyes and silently ask The Mirror to show Hunter to me. What is he doing now?

My reflection fades and I'm looking through the glass and into a room. It's a rustic room, like that of a cottage, where everything is made of wood. Cinderella is sitting on a small bed with a homespun quilt, her back against the headboard, her legs pointed straight. She's still wearing her ridiculous black dress. And Hunter is with her.

Hunter is sitting on a stool beside the bed and holding a bowl of what looks like soup. He offers it to her, and although I can't hear them, his earnest face tells me that he's trying to convince her to eat. Cinderella looks at the soup with uncaring eyes. Hunter continues to talk.

After a minute, Cinderella half-heartedly takes the bowl. Hunter looks relieved. She picks up the spoon and eats slowly, never lifting her eyes or mouthing a word. Hunter stays there and talks to her, making light gestures like he's speaking of something pleasant. At one point, Cinderella glances at him. Her lips curl up in a tired smile.

Yes, I know. He's just trying to cheer her up. But I don't like this. Hunter is *mine*. I'm not sharing him with anyone else. Least of all, her!

"I've seen enough," I say to The Mirror. The scene vanishes and my regular reflection returns. I pace in front of The Mirror while the candles sway their golden heads and my shadow crawls across the floor. The Mirror pours comfort through my body like a warm breeze but I want none of it. I want answers.

"How?" I ask sharply. "How do I get rid of her?"

The Mirror is silent for several seconds. And then a word enters my head, sharp as frostbite.

Magic.

I stop pacing.

What? I don't have magic. I don't know anyone that does, besides Cinderella. And I never saw her use it, she just told me about it. I wouldn't know where to begin.

No. Wait.... I do know where to begin. That lair in the dungeon with bottles and cauldrons and a ponderous book of spells. I peeked inside once, a few years ago, and saw Cinderella stirring something that gave off a peculiar odor. She said she tried a few spells. Some worked, some didn't.

But some *worked.*

Then there was my mother who said my beauty came from Blood Magic. She never ex-plained what that meant. But maybe... maybe she possessed magic too. And if she had it, then I might too. Such things are often hereditary.

I leave the chamber with a satisfied smile. It's time to go check out that lair.

Chapter 21

As I head downstairs, I don't hear the noise of the Dwarves anymore. I guess they finished their battle in the throne room. I stop in, just to be sure, and oh my stars, what a mess. Weapons left everywhere, swords and axes and maces and spears. The floor and walls are all scratched. Oh well. At least they left the throne in one piece–

I flinch hard. There's a *lady* in here! An old lady sitting in my throne! She slouches casually against one arm, as if she owns the place. Her legs are crossed and she swings the upper foot lightly.

"Hello, brat," she says to me.

I'm too shocked to say anything. It's kind of scary, the way she smiles at me. She's got messy gray hair done up in a sloppy bun. Wearing a worn out peasant dress with a green apron. An old lady from the villages, I guess. How on earth did she get in here?

Hesitantly, I walk toward her. "Are you one of the servants?" I ask, even though I know she isn't. She doesn't look familiar.

"Ha!" The lady says. "Do I *look* like a servant?"

"Yes, you do. Can you get out of my chair, please?"

"Why, you want it? Trust me, you won't like it. Worst thing I've ever sat on. That girl has gone plain batty."

"Who?"

"Your stepmama, the meanie-queenie."

I stop before the throne. I have to admit this old lady makes me nervous. She looks sturdy and strong, not the soft grandma type. I'm starting to think she's a mad woman who wandered into the castle.

"It's time for you to go home," I say.

"Not yet, dumpling! We're going to have a nice little talk." The lady digs inside a large pocket on the front of her apron. She brings out a little bag tied shut with a string, and then a clay pipe, long and curling.

"Are you going to smoke in here?" I ask.

"No, I'm going to play a little tune," she says dryly. She unties the bag and dumps a dark, ground substance into the bowl of the pipe. She pokes the tip of the pipe in her mouth and snaps her fingers over the bowl. Smoke begins to drift out of it.

I take a step back. "How did you do that?"

"Do what?"

"Light the pipe?"

"I snapped."

"That's not how pipes are lit."

"Oh! You're a smoker too?"

"No, but...." I sigh. "Who *are* you?"

The old lady shrugs and sucks on her pipe. "No one, really."

"Then why are you here?" My patience is really running out with this weirdo.

The old lady looks at me. "Seems like you've got some kind of problem with my Cindy."

I stare at her. "Do you mean Cinderella?"

"I do."

"You know her?"

"Did once. We're no longer speaking. But I keep an eye on her. I know about your plan to bump her off and I won't allow it. She's out of your silky-smooth, raven-black hair now. So do the girl a favor and let her be."

"Are you aware that she tried to kill me? Brutally and savagely?"

"Yeah, that was a lousy day. Poor brat wasn't herself, that stupid looking glass made her nuts. Now that's she out of this accursed palace, maybe she'll become her old self again. Not that she was ever a saint, mind you. Just let her go. She's got a nice fellow helping her out."

I bristle. "That is *my* Hunter!"

"Please, pumpkin, men are disposable. You're the queen now, you can have anybody. Give a ball and find yourself a nice fellow, I hear that works pretty well."

"I'm not the queen."

"Oh no?" The old lady eyes me from the tip of my silver tiara to the bottom of my frosty white gown. "Look at yourself."

I fold my arms. "If you care so much about Cinderella then go look after her yourself."

"Nope. Can't be done. The powers that be consider her a lost soul. I can't help her unless she changes."

I don't know what *any* of that meant. And I'm not listening to some old crone who showed up, took my chair, and filled my palace with sour smoke. "You need to go," I say firmly. "If you don't, I'll call the Dwarves and have them drag you out."

"Oh, I'd *love* to see them try that." The old lady snickers, drops her feet, and gets off the throne. She points the pipe right in my face. "Take heed, honeybun. You harm my Cindy and you won't see your next birthday. I am not your friend."

"Is that a threat?"

"Well, what would you call it, a lullaby? Just watch yourself. I'd hate to see you suffer the fate of your papa."

I gasp. "What do you know about that?"

But the old lady, humming to herself, slowly shuffles across the throne room, steering around the fallen weapons. I try to follow but suddenly my feet don't want to move. It's like they're glued to the floor.

"Hey!" I shout. "What happened to my father?"

But the old lady hums herself out of the palace, leaving a trail of gray smoke behind her.

Chapter 22

Once I can move again, I grab a torch and head down to the lair. It's at the back of the dungeon, beyond the little cells where prisoners are put. I open the heavy door and shut myself in.

There's an unhealthy smell, like dust and old moisture. The stone walls are speckled with black mold. I turn a crank on the wall which lowers a hanging rack of candles, the chain clanking and shuddering. I walk around the circular frame, lighting the candles with my torch. Then I crank it high again.

The orangey gloom reveals several tables, a large cauldron sitting in a fire pit, bottles and jars of weird substances, and a bookstand that holds an ancient-looking volume, thick as four of my fingers. I stick the torch into a bracket and turn the crackling pages. There has to be something here I can use.

Most of the spells seem petty to me. Spells that cure warts, restore lost teeth, or change the color of your eyes. I don't need any of that. The section on curses is more interesting. Sure would be fun to give Cinderella a snout like a pig. Or huge, hairy feet! She's always been obsessed with her feet, they're even smaller than mine. But no - that isn't good enough. I need something deadly.

For a minute, I think I found one. An aging curse that causes the victim to grow old and die within a week. But as I read the spell, I see it must be cast on the victim's birthday. That's seven months away for Cinderella. I can't wait that long.

I continue to search, pausing now and then to check over my shoulder. That old lady made me nervous. She clearly has magic of some kind or other. A witch, perhaps. A witch on Cinderella's side. I did not need that kind of stress.

I turn a few pages more and find a spell that somebody marked with a black feather. *Curse of Eternal Sleep,* it says. It calls for poisoning an apple with a special brew and then feeding the apple to the victim. One bite is all that's needed, and the victim will sleep forever. Not really dead, but not alive either.

I smile.

It's perfect.

The old lady doesn't want me hurting Cinderella. Very well, then. I won't hurt her. I'll just help her take a nice little nap.

Forever.

Chapter 23

I wait for Hunter by the well, as promised. For some reason, Cooper insisted on coming with me. I argued that I didn't need him – I prefer to be alone with Hunter – but he wouldn't listen. The Wood is a dangerous place, he said. The only reason I gave in is because I'm still afraid of the old lady.

I wait until long after noon. Finally, a little peasant boy I've never seen rushes into the grove with a scrap of parchment in his hand. He bows. "For you, m'lady. From Mr. Hunter."

I shake out the parchment and read it.

Snowy - The queen gave birth during the night. She is well but needs my care. I'll come to you when I am able. -H

H? How hard could it have been to write out his full name? Couldn't he have ended with some reassuring words of love? That's what *I* would have done if I had written a note. Was he in such a rush to get it over with?

I crunch the note in my fist and look at the boy. "You may tell 'H' that 'S' is not pleased. Can you remember that?"

The boy nods and, sensing my anger, runs away quickly. I stalk a circle around the grove, fuming to myself. So the child is here. At least that makes things easier. I wasn't sure if Cinderella could deliver the baby while under a sleeping curse. Now I don't have to worry.

"What happened?" Cooper asks. He's standing under an apple tree, his thick arms folded.

"Hunter isn't coming," I snap.

"All right, then let's go back."

"No. Take me to the cottage."

"I don't think that's a good idea."

"I'm not asking you to think! You'll do as I say."

"So, you're the queen now, eh?"

I sigh. Why does everyone keep saying that?

Cooper walks up to me, and without hesitation, scoops me up like a toddler. "Let's go, little miss." He tosses me over his shoulder.

"Put me DOWN!" I shout, pummeling his back with my fists. Then I notice how high I am, how the apples are right at my eyelevel. There's a big, beautiful red one hanging within my reach. I snap it off the branch before Cooper carries me away.

Chapter 24

"Mirror, Mirror, on the wall – I need to see Hunter right now."

At least The Mirror is cooperative. The scene opens up for me. I see Cinderella resting in bed, her back propped up with pillows. She looks pale and tired, but she's smiling. Her arms curl around something small, rolled in a blanket, and I can just make out the curve of a tiny red cheek. The baby. I never wanted her to see it.

Then Hunter steps into my view and sits on the stool by Cinderella's bed. At first I'm confused because Hunter is also holding a small bundle. And then I realize it's-

Another baby! Oh my stars, she had TWO!

Well, that's just peachy! Look at this mess, it's like Cinderella and I have traded places. Now I'm the Evil Queen and she gets to live in a cottage with

Hunter. They look like a sweet little family. I clench my fists until my fingernails bite into my palms. There's nothing worse than watching somebody else get everything *you* always wanted. It turns your blood to poison.

Which reminds me, I've got a curse to cook up.

I try to leave but The Mirror won't let me. A thought sinks into my head.

You're not ready.

"What?" I snap. "Just when do you think I'll *be* ready? We don't have much time. As soon as Cinderella feels better, she'll come marching back here to reclaim her throne."

The Mirror reminds me of the Dwarves.

"True," I say. "The guards are gone. I have an army now and she doesn't. But I can't stay here forever. I don't want to be the queen."

The Mirror shows me a dazzling image in which I'm sitting in the crystal throne. I'm wearing an astonishing dress made entirely of white feathers. My hair has been piled high on my head, a bouquet of black swirls behind a diamond tiara. Blood red roses are dropped in my lap and sprinkled around me on the black marble floor. It's a striking picture, though I don't understand the point of the roses. But clearly, The Mirror wants me to be the queen.

The Mirror... *wants*.

I lift my eyes to the top of The Mirror. "What are you? Why do you have feelings like a person?"

The aura begins to recede from me.

"No, don't you go away. I need to understand. You were nice to Cinderella once. And then you rejected her. Why? Was is really because you thought I was fairest? Why are you doing all this?"

Like before, a word slides into my thoughts.

Revenge.

And then the aura drops off me and I feel nothing more.

Chapter 25

Revenge? That's an interesting word. Especially coming from a thing that hangs on the wall. Why does a mirror want revenge?

I return to the scary lair and read the spell for the poisoned apple. It looks tricky. The spell must be begun at midnight and concocted in total darkness, with no light other than that of the fire below the cauldron. At first I'm worried because it calls for black rose petals which I didn't think existed. Then I find a full jar of them on a shelf. You must boil the petals for three hours in a pot of new-fallen rain, stirring once an hour while chanting the name of your victim. Several other ingredients are added, one being 'A Shriek of Despair' which I'm not sure I can pull off. Perhaps if I remember how I felt when I lost my mother.... Finally, you must soak the apple until the following midnight. If done right, the apple turns a deep purple color. Not one poisonous ingredient goes into the brew. The poison comes from the hatred in your heart.

I try. The hardest part is getting the new-fallen rain, which is needed to give the spell potency. It takes a week before we have a good downfall. I follow the instructions with scrupulous care, reading every step three times over. But after the long simmer, my apple is nothing but a squishy brown lump.

I wait for more rain and try again. The second apple boils down to nothing but skin, limp as a dead leaf.

"Why?" I rage at The Mirror. "What am I doing wrong?" The response is simply to keep trying. But I'm losing patience. Hunter and I no longer meet at the well, I've heard nothing from him since Old Cinders had her babies. I look in on them a few times but all it does is make me angry. Cinderella is very weak, she can't even stand without help. Hunter never leaves her side, often holding one baby while she tends the other. He smiles often but his face looks troubled. At night, while Cinderella sleeps, he sits by the fire with his eyes closed and his mouth pressed into his fist. I hope he is missing me terribly.

The Dwarves, meanwhile, are driving me nuts! They destroyed the palace with their mock battles, I honestly think they break things for the fun of it. And I'm getting awfully tired of having slabs of meat for supper. Sometimes they bring strange women to the palace, sometimes they light a fire and sing loud, bawdy songs while drinking tankards of ale. It's like living with a barbarian horde.

"Cooper!" I say one sunny morning that promises no new rain for my spell. "Get your brothers and meet me in the throne room. It's time to give you guys something constructive to do."

When the Dwarves assemble, I don't waste words. "This place has been Cinderella's castle for too long. She may like empty rooms and black floors but I don't. You want to break something? Fine. I want you to smash all of these marble floors. We'll replace them with something more cheerful. And let's get some new furniture, and some carpets too."

"So the queen's not coming back?" Cooper asks.

"Certainly not. I am the queen now."

"I could make some furniture," says one of the Dwarves. "I was trained as a carpenter."

"And I'm a stone mason," says another.

"Beautiful," I say. "Let's fix up the castle and then we'll have a coronation ceremony. You'll all be rewarded for helping me."

"What about Hunter?" Cooper asks.

I smile. "Hunter will be the king, of course."

The Dwarves grin. They like that idea.

"That'll make us princes!" Barker says.

"The women will come flocking," says another Dwarf. "Maybe we'll finally get some wives!"

"I want three!" Barker cries.

That makes me laugh. "Sure! Anything you want. Just fix up the palace for me. And please, no more battles."

The Dwarves agree and talk about finding tools for the project. Cooper stays with me when they leave. He follows me out of the throne room and into the parlor. "Where are you going?" he asks.

"Up to The Mirror for a while."

Cooper puts a hand on my shoulder and turns me around. "You were up there for five hours, yesterday. Give it a rest."

"I just want to talk to it."

"It's changing you."

"It's teaching me things."

"Not good things. You were nicer before."

"I am exactly the same."

Cooper points at me. "You want Hunter to like you, you gotta stay nice. You turn into some Evil Queen and he won't want you no more."

"I'm not turning into the Evil Queen! Besides, Hunter would love me no matter who I became."

"He's just a boy, not a hero. You gotta do your part."

"And what *is* my part, oh wise one?"

Cooper leans down and scowls in my face. "Stay nice!"

Chapter 26

My third attempt at the poisoned apple is a failure. This is exhausting. It's not easy staying up all night, stirring a cauldron in the dark. I have to sleep until late afternoon to recover.

"Maybe I should try something else," I say to The Mirror. I'm sitting on the floor in front of it, too exhausted to stand up. "I'm just not magical. This isn't going to work." I stare at my glum face in the glass and wait for The Mirror to respond.

It shows me a scene. A young woman, wearing a red hooded cloak, is walking through the palace garden. Snow has fallen around her, dusting the paths and dead flower beds in white. Her skin is pale, her hair is black, and at first I think the young woman is me. But as I continue to watch, I realize it's my mother.

Oh! I rise onto my knees and press my hands against the glass. My mother! I want to sob at the sight of her elegant face. I never thought I'd see it again.

She looks unhappy. The Mirror makes me understand she is grieving because she can't have a child. The first two died within her. She sits on a bench of black ebony wood, next to a bush stripped by winter to nothing but branches. Something catches her eye. A single rose blooms on this bush, red as a cherry, and sprinkled with snow. I can feel my mother's thoughts. She doesn't want the rose to die in the cold and so she tries to pluck it from the bush. But in doing so, she pricks her finger. Three drops of blood fall into the snow. My mother gazes at the beautiful red spots on their frosty carpet of white. The drops of blood glitter, bright as rubies, and my mother realizes her blood contains magic.

Carefully, my mother scoops up the droplets. Shutting her eyes, she closes her other hand over the blood and snow. "I wish I had a daughter with skin as white as snow, hair as black as ebony, and lips as red as blood." When she opens her hands, the droplets are gone. My mother smiles, knowing that somehow, her wish will come true.

So that's how I got my name. She never told me. More importantly, I know now that my mother possessed magic. It lived inside her blood. I wonder if the scary lair was once hers and if she added her blood to the spells to make them work. It makes sense. I doubt there's magic in my blood, though. I have never seen it sparkle like that. But The Mirror's message is clear. There is magic within me. I simply have to discover where it lives.

Chapter 27

Three weeks pass without a hint of rain. It doesn't matter. That curse won't work until I find the magic within me. If it exists at all. Meanwhile, I'm happy with The Mirror's company.

It shows me wonderful things. Scenes from my days as a small child when my father would kiss the tip of my nose. My mother stroking my hair and singing while I slept in her lap. Climbing into the lap of my grandfather and laughing when he tickled my face with his beard. I remember what it's like to have a family. To feel complete.

But not everything I see is enjoyable. The Mirror shows me savage arguments between my mother and father. He wanted another child, a boy to rule the kingdom. My mother, who nearly died bringing me into this world, did not. She insisted I could rule the kingdom just as well. My father wouldn't listen. He even grabbed her collar and shouted in her face. She would have a son or she would go to the devil! The crown had always passed to the male heir.

I'm beginning to miss my father much less.

As for Cinderella, she's well enough now to get out of bed. She wears a simple blue dress from the wardrobe of Hunter's mother. It looks good on her. When the babies aren't wailing, she tidies up the cottage, sweeping floors, even washing the dishes. And she looks *happy*. She begins to stitch tiny garments for the babies, and judging by the style, I think they're both girls. I didn't know Cinderella could sew.

She talks to Hunter an awful lot. Sometimes The Mirror lets me hear what they're saying. Cinderella tells him about her wicked stepmother who treated her like a servant. Hunter speaks of his family and the shame he always felt in having brothers that were thieves. How he hopes one day they will follow his example and choose to work for a living.

He never told me that.

Then there's one evening when Cinderella is sitting on her bed while the babies sleep beside her. Hunter comes in with a small cake of some kind. He rips it in two and gives half to Cinderella. A few crumbs drop onto his vest, so he brushes them off with his hand. As he does, the top button of his vest snaps off and bounces across the floor. Hunter laughs as he retrieves it, holds it up to show Cinderella, and slips the button onto a shelf.

Cinderella puts her cake aside. She gestures at the button and speaks with a sweet smile. Hunter stares at her, looking astonished. He removes his vest, grabs the button off the shelf, and takes them to her. She digs a needle and thread out of a drawer in her bedside table. And then she sits there, drawing the needle up and down, and sews the button back on.

Hunter's face is strange as he watches her. He's not smiling but his eyes are very soft. When she hands back the vest, he nods a thank-you and strokes the button with his thumb. Touched. He looks touched.

I blow the air out of my cheeks. There are definite disadvantages to having a sensitive man.

"Maybe I went about this the wrong way," I say to The Mirror. "Hunter didn't want to kill Cinderella. I wouldn't listen and now he's afraid to come back. I love Hunter. I shouldn't have tried to make him do something against his nature. I'll go to him and agree to his plan. Cinderella can be the queen again and keep her babies. And Hunter and I will go far away. So long as I'm with him, nothing else matters."

The Mirror's tone becomes sterner. I must be the queen. It is my destiny. I can't give that up for the sake of a boy. Cinderella must be destroyed.

"Why should you want to kill Cinderella?" I ask hotly. "You loved her once and now you want her dead? You nearly killed *me* when I was a child! Just what are you, some kind of demon?"

I try to walk away but it holds me fast. It shows me another image of myself as queen but I squeeze my eyes shut. I won't let it tell me who I am or what I do. I can feel The Mirror becoming angry.

Something grips my waist and I'm lifted off the floor. I hear a gruff voice but can't tell what it's saying. My head feels heavy and fogged. After a minute, I realize Cooper is carrying me down the stairs. He takes me to the white sitting room and drops me onto the chaise lounge.

"I heard you talking," Cooper says. "When I looked in, your eyes were shut and you were shaking all over. You told me to drag you away if you did anything weird."

"Thank you," I say weakly. I lean my head into both of my hands. The sudden rip away from The

Mirror has left me cold and sick. It wants me to come back, I can feel that from here.

"Cooper... will you please take me to your cottage? I need to see Hunter, it's very important."

Cooper pats my knee. "Rest a bit, little miss. That infernal thing has made you tired. We can go another day."

I look at him, suddenly suspicious. "Why do you keep refusing me? Every time I ask to go to the cottage, you give me some excuse."

Cooper shrugs. "Best if you stay here, I think."

"Does this have anything to do with Hunter? Did he tell you to keep me away from him?"

"No." That's all he says. Too quick, too short.

I sit straighter. "I want to know what he said."

"Fine, but you won't like it. He spoke to Barker the night we sent him to check the cottage. Hunter thinks you and the queen should be kept apart. Says you might kill each other if you're together. He asked us to keep you here at the castle, and he's trying to keep the queen where she is. Just until things are settled."

"How dare you!" I jump up from the lounge. "All this time I thought you were my friends!"

"We are, you little lunatic. You just don't know what's good for you."

"I'm leaving. Now! And you won't stop me." I stalk to the door but Cooper simply blocks me and folds his arms. "Well, that was easy."

I grind my teeth. "So I'm a prisoner here?"

"Until Hunter says otherwise, yes. Now come on, little miss, don't make a fuss. We did some good work on the castle, gave the throne room a nice granite floor. Barker is building you a new chair, I think you'll like it. Just take a look and forget about Hunter for a while."

I wish I could hurl him across the room. I *hate* being small and fragile like this, I have no power! And if I throw a fit he might lock me up in the dungeons. So I'll have to play along. But no one, not even Hunter, gets to make me a prisoner. I will find a way to that cottage myself.

I'll just have to be sneaky about it.

Chapter 28

That night, my dreams are filled with Hunter. I remember the day I met him in The Wood. I released a rabbit that was caught in a trap and I heard someone laugh and say, "That's my supper you just set free." I was haughty to him at first, unaccustomed to friends of any kind. But when I left, he said, "Will you come back tomorrow?" And that changed everything.

A month later he kissed me for the first time. He told me the trees whispered secrets when the wind blew, and if I closed my eyes, I would hear them. To humor him, I closed my eyes. And then I felt his lips. His arms came next, closing us in a tight circle, and when we were through, he said, "The secret is that I love you, Snowy."

I wake up with tears sliding into my pillow. Oh my Hunter! I will get you back!

I rise although the sun has not. I throw a dress over my head and strap on the belt and dagger. It's a long, dark walk from my tower room to The Mirror's chamber. But I have a plan that I think will work.

"Tell me where this cottage is," I say to The Mirror. "I will go there and stab Cinderella in her sleep. Then I'll bring Hunter back here with me. That way, both of us are getting what we want. But first I need to know where he lives."

The Mirror doesn't believe me. It can see through the lie, that I'm not really planning on killing Cinderella.

"I caaan't!" I whine. "Hunter will never forgive me if I do. I know that for sure. I'm sorry, Mirror! But I love Hunter more than you."

A scene opens before me. The Mirror holds me in place and makes me watch. I see my mother, my beautiful mother, standing before this very mirror. She tucks a few stray hairs into place and she is smiling. She wears a gown of garnet red that exposes her throat and shoulders. My father comes into the room behind her.

"Where is Snow White?" my father asks.

"Having her lessons," my mother says, tugging down the sleeves of her dress. Her face and voice have turned cold. "I'm going out for a bit."

"Hmm. I'd like you to stay," my father says. He takes hold of my mother's waist from behind and kisses the side of her neck. My mother stiffens. "There will be no other child, Edgar. You are wasting your time."

My father meets her eyes in the mirror and his face has become strangely calm. "No, my dear. You have wasted *your* time in not providing a son for me. I have been patient. But I'm afraid your time is up." His hands lift off my mother's waist and wrap around her throat.

I gasp.

My mother gasps too and her hands fly to her neck. She tries to pry off his fingers, her mouth wide open, then she throws back her hands and claws at his face. My father shifts and bends over her, forcing her to crouch, and they sink to the floor while my mother makes little grunts and gasps, and her face darkens red as her dress. He presses her down, holding her with the weight of his body, while her feet scrape the floor and her hands reach for help with splayed fingers. One flying hand strikes the hard edge of the mirror's frame and moments later I see blood on her palm. Her whole body jerks and shudders, her face squished up in a soundless scream. My father's teeth are bared as he struggles to squeeze her throat. Suddenly, my mother turns her head and presses her bloody hand to the mirror. Her lips move like a fish out of water, but I can see she's mouthing words. Then her hand slips downward, leaving a bloody streak on the glass. Her limbs stop quivering. My father waits another minute before walking away, leaving my dead mother in front of the mirror.

Chapter 29

I crawl into a corner and throw up. Still sobbing, still shaking, I return to The Mirror and sit against it, leaning my head on the glass. Oh my poor, poor mother! I never knew! My father told me she died because of trouble with her lungs. I guess that was true. She couldn't use her lungs when he was strangling her!

I press my cold, trembling hands to the glass and feel the love pour into me like warm syrup. She is here now. In her final moments, she managed a spell that transported her life essence. My mother *became* The Mirror. She's been here all this time, waiting for me to grow up. Waiting to help me become the queen I was always meant to be.

I ask why she nearly killed me when I looked in The Mirror as a child. She helped me understand that she needed Cinderella then, drew power from her constant worship. Cinderella thought The Mirror loved only her and so it had to look as if The Mirror didn't want me. But she would not have let me harm myself. She sum-moned my father to pull me off the window sill. He was unaware my mother still lived in the mirror and so she could manipulate him in small ways.

On my sixteenth birthday, The Mirror rejected Cinderella. It threw out a force of hate so strong that Cinderella was knocked on her back and across the floor. She went wild with grief as she realized The Mirror would never want her again. Cinderella never knew who The Mirror truly was. Only that it was something that made her feel loved.

I cry until I have strength for no more. I nearly fall asleep on the floor but The Mirror reminds me I have a job to do. I get up and wipe my swollen eyes. Of course I will kill Cinderella. She had no right to take my mother's place. I will avenge my dear mother and become the next queen. Hunter will have to understand.

Finally, The Mirror shows me the Dwarves' cottage. It sits in a distant part of The Wood, segregated from the nearest village. The cottage looks like the Dwarves, big and rustic. It's got two floors, a timber frame and stone walls, and a thatched roof like a hood of messy hair. The shutters are crooked and one window is broken, but otherwise it all looks sturdy and solid. The Mirror tells me which roads I must take to get there.

I return to my little tower room to fetch a shawl. Then I tiptoe down through the dark palace, holding my breath whenever I pass a snoring Dwarf. The Mirror assured me it could hold them in sleep for a little while. I sure hope they won't come after me when they wake up, especially Cooper. Hopefully, he won't realize I'm gone and just assume I'm with The Mirror.

I slip out of the palace through a side door because the big ones in front are too groany. The sky is deep-water blue but the edges are paling. I unfold my shawl of white wool, drape it over my head, and hug it to my body. The hanging folds conceal the jeweled dagger on my hip. I must look like a ghost as I cross the palace grounds and weave between the trees of The Wood. I walk slowly and methodically, without looking back. Today I am an angel of death. I will return Cinderella to the ashes from which she came.

It's a long, lonely walk. Far past the cave that leads to my tower. Someday, I'll go back there, at least for a while. It's good to have a secret place where the horrible world can't find you.

I'm still sickened by the memory of my mother's murder. Devastated to learn my father was such a monster. Did he even think about what he was taking from me? Why do some parents think their own children don't matter, that their feelings are somehow inferior? What-ever that assassin lady did to my father, he deserved much worse. I hope she beat him to death with a hot poker.

Speaking of hot pokers, the sky has become a nice fiery orange. The sleepy silence of The Wood has been replaced by chirpy birds. I'm moving through a patch of forest with stripes of slender birch trees when I see the cottage at last. Suddenly, all of this becomes very real.

I hover behind the trees, afraid to be seen. The cottage looks so peaceful and warm, glowing in the buttery light of morning. I clutch the dagger beneath my shawl and try to calm my stomping heart. It's not easy to just walk into someone's house and stab them with a knife. This is bound to give me some scarring memories.

"Hello, brat."

I shriek and whirl around. The old lady is back! She's wearing a heavy brown cloak with a hood around her face and the pipe pokes out of the hollow. She grins and her stained, yellow teeth are disgusting.

"Up early today, aren't you?" she says.

I drop my hand from my mouth to my chest and lean against the nearest birch tree. "Oh my stars, you *scared* me! Where did you come from?"

"I followed you. Looked like you were up to no good and I see I'm right. That knife's not for cutting a birthday cake, is it?"

I draw out the dagger and hold it up for her to see. "No, it isn't. And you better leave now before you become the cake."

"Ha!" Her sudden laugh blows a gust of smoke in my face. I cough and swat at the air while the old lady cackles. I really wish I had the power to scare people.

"Nice try, pumpkin-pie. Now listen up! I've come to make a bargain with you."

"What bargain is that?"

The old lady draws something out from under her cloak and holds it before my face. It's an apple, plump and pretty, and pink as a carnation. "Leave my Cindy alone," she says. "And you can have this."

I stare at it, awestruck. It's too pink to be natural. Which means it's enchanted. And I know of only one spell that makes an apple turn pink.

"Is that-?"

"Yep. A Love Apple."

I draw my breath. A Love Apple! I had all but forgotten. This will solve everything between me and Hunter, make him stay with me forever. I reach for the apple with trembling fingers. I knew the old lady had magic, I knew it!

She pulls back. "First you must promise not to harm my Cindy. Give me the dagger to prove it. And everlasting love will be yours! Isn't that what you want?"

I bite my lip. Yes, that's what I want. More than anything. Hunter loving me forever, even if it's enchanted. I would rather have artificial love than an all-natural heartbreak.

"Sure, yes, fine," I say, anything to get that apple. The old lady smiles and drops it into my hand. "All yours, tootsie. Take it to your honey. But remember! The lady has to bite first."

I nod quickly though I don't remember that part. But I did read the spell only once. "Thank you." I hold out the dagger, blade downward. The old lady takes it and smirks. "Sweet dreams, angel-face." She pokes the pipe in her mouth and walks away from me, chuckling to herself.

I hurry up the path to the cottage door, grinning like a fool. This is so perfect! First, Hunter and I will bite the apple. Then I'll take his hunting knife and kill Cinderella. He can't hate me for it once he's under the love spell. The Mirror and I will both get what we want. As for the old lady, I'm sure The Mirror can tell me how to handle her. The Mirror can do anything.

I'm lifting my hand to knock on the door when suddenly it swings open. And there is Cinderella, standing right in front of me.

Chapter 30

"Snow White?"

"Hi."

"What are you doing here?"

"I... came to see Hunter."

"Oh. He's not here." Cinderella doesn't budge from the doorway. She's carrying a fat basket that appears to be full of laundry.

I drop my hand to my side, under the shawl, and hope she won't notice the apple. "Do you know when he's coming back?"

"Soon, I think." She just stands there, staring at me, not inviting me in. It's so rude.

I clear my throat. "So... how are the babies?"

"Good. I was coming out to hang their clothes before they wake up."

I smirk. "I don't remember you doing stuff like that."

"I did before... before I became the queen." Cinderella sighs. "Come with me." She leads me around the house to a little yard in the back. It's mostly dirt, with weeds and wild flowers growing at the edges. There's a clothesline strung from the house to a wooden pole, and a table with benches for eating outside.

She plops the basket beneath the clothesline and lifts out a tiny white gown. "What have you been doing?"

I shrug. "Stuff."

"At the palace?"

"Yeah."

"And talking to The Mirror?"

I hesitate. Cinderella narrows her eyes at me. "Yes, I can see you have. I suppose you want to be queen now, don't you?"

"Maybe."

Cinderella pins the little gown on the line. Her face looks peaceful. "You can have it if you want. I'm not going back there." She closes her eyes momentarily. "You know, once, I wanted to be the queen. And I got what I wanted. But it wasn't what I wanted." She looks at me and almost smiles. "I don't hate you anymore, Snowy."

"You don't want to be the Evil Queen?"

"Not anymore. I think I'd rather be queen of somebody's heart than queen of a kingdom."

I don't like the sound of that. Cinderella bends down to fetch another garment. As she stands up, the wind catches the folds of my shawl and exposes my hand for a moment. "What's that?" Cinderella asks.

Rats! She saw the apple. "Oh... it's nothing." I show it to her, hoping that will seem natural. "Just an apple."

"It's pink." Cinderella's eyes widen. "Is that the Love Apple?"

I cover it with my other hand. "No."

"It is. I can tell."

"It's for me and Hunter," I mumble, stroking the glossy pink skin. "Did you know that my mother was killed by my father?"

Cinderella blinks. "I – yes."

"You never told me."

"Would you have wanted to know?"

I look down without answering. I guess she's right. Who wants to know something like that?

"Where'd Hunter go?" I ask softly. "Maybe I can find him."

Cinderella bends down, picks up another little dress, and pins it on the line before speaking.

"You're going to ask him to bite the apple, aren't you?"

"That was the general idea."

Cinderella looks at me and there's turbulence in her eyes. She's struggling with something.

"He's a good man, Snowy. Kind and gentle and thoughtful. I like him very much."

"Thanks, I like him too." But I don't like this conversation. Something bad is brewing, I know it.

Cinderella blows the air from her cheeks and slouches a little. Then she straightens up and faces me. "I want you to let me have him."

"Um, what?"

"He's the first man in so long who treats me well. I'm not willing to give that up. You're young and pretty, you can find someone else." She holds out her hand, the fingers curled upward. "So please, give me the apple. I get Hunter and you get to be queen. Do we have a deal?"

I glare at her. "NOT... a chance."

Cinderella's lips press together. Her blue eyes harden. "I would like the apple, Snow White."

"You can't *have* it, Cinderella."

She hesitates for half a second. Then her hands shoot out and seize the apple. I gasp and jump back but her hands are over mine. She yanks my arms straight.

"NO!" I jerk the apple back to my chest but Cinderella comes with it. She tries to dig her nails under my fingers and peel them off. Her teeth are bared.

"Let it GO, Stepchild!" she growls.

"You can't...have...EVERYTHING!" I shriek. I try shaking the apple out of her grasp. "He's MY Hunter!"

"You don't need him!" Cinderella shouts. We stagger across the yard, wrestling around the apple which is almost entirely concealed by our hands. I kick Cinderella's shins. She curses and swings me around her, trying to snap me off with a whiplash motion.

"I should've killed you when you were a child!" Cinderella shouts.

"I should've killed *you* the day you became queen!" I shout back.

We grapple around the apple, our elbows high. I push against Cinderella, forcing her across the yard until her back hits the wall of the cottage. We're both breathless, shiny with sweat. But I think Cinderella is tiring. She just had two babies, after all. Her face looks more distressed than angry.

She shifts, lifting her knee, and I feel a tiny foot against my stomach. Then she kicks out, hard, and I'm thrown back, flat on the dirt. I lie there, stunned, my arms spread out like wings. She did it. She beat me. Cinderella gets every-thing she wants with her freaking feet!

I try to sit up but my stomach cramps with pain. Cinderella lifts the apple and bites a chunk out of it. She smiles at me as she chews. "You lose, Stepchild. You will always lose to me."

I call her something I can't repeat.

Cinderella frowns. At first I think it's because of my insult, but then she lifts a hand to her throat. She blinks several times and turns the apple to look at the bite mark. The flesh inside is a deep purple color.

I manage to stand, my mouth hanging open. "Is – is that...?"

Cinderella drops, smooth and soft as a flower wilting. The apple rolls out of her hand.

Chapter 31

I back away from her, covering my mouth. The apple! It was *poisoned!* The old lady – she meant it for me. To stop me from harming her precious Cindy. It would have worked, too, if Cinderella had been less selfish. A shiver crawls up my spine as I realize how close I came.

"Snowy?"

I spin around. Hunter emerges from the forest, holding an armload of firewood. His eyes shift from me to Cinderella on the ground. He gasps. "Snowy! What did you do?"

"She did it herself!" I cry. "She bit the apple, I didn't know it was poisoned!" My eyes sting with tears. He doesn't even look happy to see me. And it's been almost a month!

Hunter drops the firewood and runs past me. He crouches by Cinderella. She's lying on her side, the arm that held the apple stretched out before her. He holds his fingers underneath her nose and then touches her cheek. "She's breathing," he says. "But she's cold."

I nod, clutching my hands together. They're chilled and throbbing, the fingernails blue. I don't know why my hands do this when I'm upset.

"What do we do?" Hunter looks at me with worried eyebrows.

"We can't do anything," I say. "She's under a spell. She's not dead but she's... never going to wake up."

Hunter's mouth falls open. "Snowy! How could you do this?"

"I didn't!"

"Then how'd it happen? Why are you here?"

"I came to see YOU!" I shout.

"Not exactly, dumpling. She came to kill Cindy and *then* see you," says a voice that's not mine or Hunter's. There's a burst of color and the weird old lady is standing in the yard with us. Only now she looks very different. She's wearing a fancy green dress, like a ball gown, though it's kind of tattered and wrinkly. Her gray hair is caught up like a bush on top of her head. And she's got two, thin silvery wings that fan out from her back.

The old lady is a fairy.

She looks once at Cinderella and the face she turns on me is sheer hatred. "Little beast!" She thrusts out her hand, pointing the tip of her pipe right at me. A gust of sparkles shoots out, hits my chest, and I'm thrown topsy-turvy across the yard. I land hard, skidding across the dirt with my feet in the air.

The old lady marches toward me. "Why didn't you just bite it, you wretch!"

"I was! I was!" I skitter back on the ground, lifting an arm to block myself. "She fought me for it, didn't you see?"

"Hey!" I hear Hunter's voice from behind her. "Leave Snowy alone! Just who are you supposed to be?"

"I'm Cinderella's fairy godmother!" The old lady watches me with blazing eyes. "Call me 'Godnutter' if you want – that's what she did. Didn't she ever speak of me?"

"Well – yes, a little." My voice is high. "But you – you made me think that was a Love Apple! You tricked me!"

"'Course I did. Just like I tricked your miserable father. All I needed was a pretty face and he followed me right up to that nasty little tower."

I gasp. "You were the beautiful lady?"

"I was. I asked your father a simple question. He gave the wrong answer, and I punished him. I left one of my pipes behind in the tower so Cindy would know I had been there."

"So you killed him." It really doesn't matter to me now.

"Oh, he's alive, dearie. But don't go looking for him, you won't find him."

"He's alive?" I stand up.

"Not important now!" Godnutter snaps. She points at Cinderella. "Do me a favor and get her off the ground. I'm going to see if I can fix this."

And she vanishes.

Chapter 32

Hunter and I stare at each other, speechless.

"Let's uh, put her on the table," Hunter says. "In case that lady wants to... I don't know, work on her."

I nod. We drag the long wooden table out to the middle of the yard. Looks like it was once red but most of the paint has chipped off. Then we carry Cinderella and drape her over the top. I tug down and straighten her pale blue dress. She looks pretty, sleeping there. Like a doll made of sugar.

Hunter runs his fingers through his hair and glances back at the cottage. "I should check on the babies."

"I'll do it," I say, because I don't want to keep standing there. I walk round to the front of the house and let myself in the little door. The cottage looks familiar, thanks to my Mirror spying. It doesn't take me long to find the room Cinderella used. There's the bed with the patchwork quilt. Near the corner of the bed, close to the wall, two infants are sleeping, curled into each other. So impossibly small it almost hurts me to look at them. Such a frightening, fragile way to enter this brutal world.

I return to the yard. "They're fine," I tell Hunter. He stands a few feet back from the table, watching Cinderella. I creep over to stand at his side. I wonder if this would be a bad time to try and kiss him. He looks so tempting, his brown hair ruffled from running his fingers through it, his sleeves pushed up to the elbows, baring his smooth arms. I ache to have him all around me.

I start to reach for his hand. Then Godnutter pops back in sight, on the other side of the table. She stares at Cinderella, smoking and scowling.

"Well?" Hunter asks.

Godnutter shakes her head. "Not good. She needs a kiss to wake her up. The poisoned apple was made with true hate-" she glares at me "-so only true love can cure it. She needs to be kissed by someone that loves her."

I can't help it. I giggle.

"What's so funny?" Godnutter asks sharply.

"What's funny is that she will never wake up!" I say, laughing. "Because absolutely nobody loves Cinderella!"

Hunter bows his head and closes his eyes. He folds his arms tightly and heaves a long sigh.

"I do."

I turn and look at him. He looks back at me, soft and sad. "I'm sorry, Snowy. I really am. But I can't help it."

"What are you saying?" I ask.

Hunter's eyes drift away from me and settle on Cinderella. "I love her," he whispers.

Tears wash over me instantly. "Hunter... that's impossible. You love *me* and no one else. You told me that!"

"I know." Hunter's face looks anguished. "But... now I love her. I didn't try, it just happened. I think – I think I can wake her up."

I draw my breath. "You're going to kiss her?"

Hunter looks at her. And nods.

I clench my fists, my chest heaving. I won't allow this! Hunter has kissed no other girl but me!

"She's not *good* for you, Hunter!" I shout. "She's a bad person! Selfish and nasty and mean!"

Godnutter cracks a laugh. "She is, you know."

"She was improving," Hunter says. "She needed someone to be kind to her, that's all. She needed to be loved."

"What, and I *don't* need to be loved?" I cry.

"I *did* love you!" Hunter says, louder now.

"Oh, but now you love her!" I jab a finger at Cinderella. "And what's made her so special, hmm? Is she prettier than me?"

Hunter steps toward me. He looks right in my face. "She sewed a button."

I stare at him. "What?"

He points at the top button of his vest. "It fell off one night. She offered to sew it back on. She offered."

I scowl at him. "So?"

Hunter starts to pace. He looks worked up. "So, when did you ever do *anything* for me? I didn't *want* to steal the baby! I didn't *want* to kill the queen! None of that mattered to you. You just wanted me to worship you and carry out your commands! You never asked me what I wanted."

"He's got a point, pumpkin," Godnutter says.

"Well, what *do* you want?" I snap.

Hunter folds his arms. "Right now? I want Cinderella."

My face squishes up and I cry. My Hunter! He is my first thought when I wake in the morning, my last before I fall asleep. Everything I did, I did for us. How could this happen? All of this over one lousy button?

Hunter turns away from me. He steps toward the table where Cinderella lies, stiff and pale as a corpse. He gently slides his fingers under her hand.

I'm breathing heavily. And I realize something. This is all The Mirror's fault. The Mirror kept me away from Hunter. It wouldn't tell me where the cottage was. It wanted me to use magic to get rid of Cinderella, so I wasted precious time trying to make a poisoned apple. It convinced me I had to be the queen, something I never even wanted. And all that time, Old Cinders was working her evil charms on Hunter. I fell prey to The Mirror, just like she did. I let it control me.

I would much rather have Hunter, warm and loving, than the ghost of a dead mother behind a piece of glass.

Hunter pushes a delicate strand of hair off Cinderella's face. He leans in toward her lips.

I put out my hands. "Hunter, wait!"

He stops and looks at me.

I wipe my eyes and try to stop whimpering. "C-can you do one more thing for me? Just one more thing? And then I'll... I'll let you go."

"What is it?" Hunter asks softly. I can see he feels sorry for me.

"I need you to destroy The Mirror."

Chapter 33

We walk through the forest, back toward the palace. The sun is high now, the sky blue as a jewel. We have to bring the babies with us. I'm carrying one, wrapped in a thin green blanket, while Hunter carries the other. Godnutter stayed behind to watch over her sleeping beauty.

"Why can't one of those big fellows bash the looking glass?" she asked with a scowl. I shook my head at her. I want Hunter to save me. And I want him to punish The Mirror.

We don't talk. I stare at the baby cradled in my arms. She's so perfect, with cheeks soft as a sigh, and a feathery fluff of red hair. The baby Hunter holds has brown hair. My little sisters. I wonder if Cinderella will ever let me see them.

It feels strange, awful, walking beside Hunter without speaking to him. I don't know what to do,

I just don't. Once he breaks The Mirror, he'll go back to Cinderella. And what about me? I'll just be the stupid queen. Sitting in that big empty throne room with nothing but the dopey Dwarves for company. I don't care about the kingdom. I don't care about the people. I just want Hunter!

We leave The Wood behind us and cross over the palace grounds. My shawl fell off during my tussle with Cinderella, leaving my arms uncovered. The wind swoops over me, whispering a chill into my skin. A foretelling of frost to come.

I climb the palace steps first. Cooper must have seen us coming because he's waiting at the top. He looks grouchy and his beard is tangled.

"Came back, did you?" he says gruffly. "We were all set to go out and look for you."

"I'm fine," I say. Boy, what a lie that is. "I brought Hunter to do something for me."

Cooper nods a greeting at Hunter. Then he looks at the babies. "Is the queen dead?"

Hunter and I shake our heads. It's too much to explain.

We pass him and enter the main corridor of the palace. The other Dwarves are waiting there, each holding a huge weapon. Like they really need those to look for me. By our faces, I think they can tell something's up because when I turn into the parlor, they follow.

The Mirror – my mother – is angry. She knows. We're not even on the stairs yet and I can feel the thick aura of rage. My heart starts to squirm. I press the baby into my chest and push against the fog of fury. This has to be done. With The Mirror gone, maybe I can win Hunter back. Become again the Snowy he loved. But that won't happen so long as The Mirror continues to rule my life.

Hunter lifts a foot onto the bottom step and stops. He turns to me, startled. "Oh my goodness." He can feel it.

I nod, my mouth dry and sticky. "Try to ignore it. Don't listen."

Hunter works his way up the stairs, the baby on his front, the crossbow on his back. I keep close behind him but every step is harder. It's like trying to swim upstream through a torrent of filthy water. First my stomach sickens, then my head pounds, then my feet become heavy as lead. The baby in my arms grows restless and makes whimpering noises.

Traitor.

The word enters my mind like a blade. It soaks into me, bone deep, heavy as sin. I am betraying my own mother. The person who gave life to me. I deserve to be hanged by the neck from a tree and have crows pick at my flesh.

Ahead of me, Hunter sways and catches the railing. For a moment I see the side of his face and it's sparkling with sweat. I wonder what she's telling *him*.

"Fight it!" I hiss through my teeth. "It's only a mirror!"

"It's a demon," Cooper says. I twist back to look at him and his rugged face has gone pale. So have the other Dwarves. But they're not shaking like me and Hunter. Maybe The Mirror is just focusing on the two of us. Or maybe the Dwarves are just bigger and stronger. I don't know, but either way, they look less affected.

"*Help* us!" I whisper.

Cooper steps behind me and takes hold of my shoulders. Barker goes ahead and puts a hand on Hunter's back. Together, they push us to the top of the stairs.

The chamber lies ahead, double doors hanging open. For one short moment, I see The Mirror, its moaning mouth of dusty glass surrounded by the dark golden frame. Then the doors swing on their own and shut with a heart-stopping *BANG!*

The babies jump and break into frantic crying.

Chapter 34

On the landing, Hunter and I lean against the nearest wall. I try to calm the baby by patting her back, but she cries, harshly and jaggedly, her little tongue suspended in her mouth. The sound cuts through my head like a saw.

"Stay there!" Cooper shouts. He takes his club, the heavy one with spikes on the end, and steps in front of the doors. He lifts, swings, and drops the club on the door handles. *CRACK!* The handles break and fall to the floor.

Cooper raises a booted foot and kicks the doors open. "There! Let's get this done." I guess he's figured out what we came to do. It's pretty obvious.

The Dwarves troop into the room first. I wait and watch but they don't get incinerated or drop stone-dead. So I hoist the wailing baby higher and walk into the room. It still feels like I'm wading through a lake of tar.

Worthless.

The next word crushes down on me. I can barely stand. I am nothing, nothing at all. No beauty, no talents, no intelligence. The unwanted daughter of a wicked king. I should throw myself from the highest tower and end our disgraceful line.

Hunter is beside me, his face clenched with pain. "Take her!" he says. I barely have time to shift the first baby before he transfers the second one into my arms. He lifts the shoulder strap of his crossbow and swings the weapon around to his front. "I'm going to shoot it."

My arms are shaking. I can't hold both babies, not in my state. I crouch and carefully lay the babies on the floor by the wall, using their blankets to cushion them a little. It seems harsh but still better than dropping them. And I can't trust the Dwarves to hold them gently.

I'm on my hands and knees, laying out the second baby, when I feel a burst of power from The Mirror. Hunter's thrown right off his feet and hits the wall behind him. The air around me tightens like a fist and I shriek as I'm sucked across the floor on my hands and knees. Fingernails scraping marble, I'm dragged in front of The Mirror. It spins me around to face it.

Stand!

I can't disobey. I lift one wobbly leg, then the other. Trembling all over, I look into The Mirror.

There she is. My mother. She fills the glass, top to bottom, larger than life. She's wearing the same blood-red gown she had on when my father killed her. It flaps around her as if blown by the wind, and her long black hair ripples behind her. Her beautiful eyes blaze at me, burning with dark fire.

"Ungrateful child!" she cries.

I stand there sobbing. I can't stop. Everything she says drops straight into my soul and becomes part of me.

"You would destroy your own mother?" she shouts. "Look at me! Look at what he did!" She lifts her chin and shows me the ring of dark bruises around her neck, left by my father's fingers.

"I'm sorry!" I cry. "I really am! But he's gone now! You need to stop using me for your revenge."

"You *will* be queen!" she says savagely. "And nothing else! I have waited too long for this!"

"I don't want to be the queen! I'm not you! I want to be me!"

"And *who* are *you*, Snow White? Nothing but a bratty child. Even that silly boy no longer wants you. You have no one but me now!"

"That's YOUR fault!" I shout. Tears are pouring down my face. My hands ache so much with cold I can barely move my fingers and the throbbing chill has spread up to my elbows. "You're no better than Cinderella! No better than my father! You're all just EVIL! I don't want any of you!"

My mother stares at me, her hair dipping and swirling across her face. She's so angry she looks more scary than beautiful, her pale skin tight on her bones.

"You are *my* child!" she says. "You belong to *me!* If you won't embrace the life I've given you, then I can take it back. I will *not* be abandoned!"

I gasp as I'm yanked forward, thrust flat against the mirror. I catch myself with both hands and they're so frozen they mist up the glass. My whole body is squashed against the surface. And immediately I feel weakened, heavy with fatigue.

"You will suffer as I have, you wretched girl!" my mother says. "I will draw you in here with me!"

My vision blurs, my limbs shake. She's taking my energy, all of it at once. I'm going to die within seconds. And then she'll pull my essence into the mirror and I'll be trapped there with her. Forever.

From far away, worlds away, I hear a familiar voice. "Snowy! Drop!"

I look at my hands on the glass, try to focus on them. And I push. My body pitches straight back and I hit the floor like a felled tree. Then comes the explosion: a high, twinkling, burst of glass; a rush of white fragments flying over me; a musical rain of bright slivers. And then it's quiet. The mirror is nothing but a blank wooden oval with a frame around it. An arrow from Hunter's crossbow is embedded at the center.

Chapter 35

I roll over, push up on my elbows. The fog in my head begins to clear. The babies wail harder, sounding terrified. And the Dwarves look shocked. My eyes travel up the floor ahead of me, littered with jagged shards of the mirror. But not as many as there should be. I look ahead and I'm staring at the bottoms of Hunter's boots.

I gasp. "HUNTER!"

I scramble over to him on all fours. He's on his back, the crossbow dropped near his feet. Dark patches of blood are leaching through his clothes. They cover his legs, his chest, his arms, and fresh gashes bleed from his neck and face. When he shot The Mirror, she hurled her fragments at him. Stabbed him all over his body. Hunter's gentle brown eyes stare at the ceiling, blank as stone.

I stare at him. I can't breathe.

My Hunter... my Hunter....

He's gone.

I grip the sides of my head and scream, loud enough to split the walls. I draw my breath and scream again, bowing down to the floor. I drop one hand to the marble and the pain bursts out of me and I hear a sharp crackle. I open my eyes. A layer of ice has spread out like a star around me, nearly the width of the room. The dead center is where my hand touched the floor.

I just found the magic within me.

I look up at the Dwarves, stunned, my eyes coated with tears. I blink to clear them. The seven Dwarves are all staring at me. There's not one friendly face among them.

"You just killed our brother, you witch," Cooper growls.

"No!" I squeak out.

Cooper turns back to his brothers, all grim-faced and clenching their axes and clubs.

"Kill her," Cooper says.

"NO!" I scream. I lurch forward and smack my other hand to the floor while directing my gaze at the Dwarves. A path of ice shoots across the floor and slides up the Dwarves' legs to their knees. I stare, focusing my fear on them, and the ice thickens. They can't move.

I lift my hand off the floor, gaping. I can't believe that worked!

I jump up, avoiding the slippery ice. I sprint over the floor and stoop to pick up the babies, first one, then the other. The Dwarves are cursing and straining their legs against the ice. I know it won't hold them for long.

I rush out of the room and down the stairs, fast as I dare, considering I'm carrying two infants with wobbly heads. The jostling distracts them from crying for the moment. But they're heavy for me. I don't know how I'll outrun the Dwarves this way. And if they catch me, they'll kill us all.

I get out of the palace. I don't take the gravel drive that leads out to the towns, it's too open. I cut through the palace gardens, dried up and dying with the approach of autumn. The Wood lies ahead of me, a rough wall of trees. I hurry across the grass, anxious to reach the shelter of its shadows. I'm nearly there.

BOOM! Godnutter pops right in front of me.

"Well!" she barks. "Fine mess YOU'VE made of things! Who's going to save my Cindy now?" She's got her hands on her hips, so angry she's not even smoking.

"Godnutter, please!" I cry. "Please help me! I have to get away from here, they're going to kill me!"

"And it would serve you right, wouldn't it? I didn't come to save you, tootsie. I came to lighten your load." She swoops in and scoops a baby out of my arms, the one with brown hair. She steps back. "This one's mine."

My eyes widen. "NO!"

"She wanted a fairy to protect her baby, didn't she? Well, here I am! I want another chance at this."

"Give her back, she's my sister!"

"Not any more. And you don't have time to argue, those fellows are breaking out of that ice." She shifts the baby to her left arm and with her right thrusts deep into the pocket of her dress. She yanks out the pipe and points the tip at me. "Hold still."

I gasp as she fires a river of sparkles at my chest. I step back, my breasts warm and tingling, and look down. They're swollen like two melons and feel heavy.

"What did you just do?" I cry.

"Gave you the means to feed the baby, you cow! Now off with you! Get her to safety!" Godnutter vanishes and the brown-haired baby with her.

I tuck the red-haired baby against me, her fuzzy head just under my chin. And I run into The Wood.

I know exactly where I'm going.

Chapter 36

I break out of the cave into the meadow with the tower. There it stands, sturdy and gray, the home I planned for me and Hunter. My hopes and dreams a shattered mess, just like The Mirror. I can hardly bear to look at it.

The baby sleeps on my shoulder, worn out from crying. I didn't hear the Dwarves behind me as I ran. But they will come. This clearing is hard to find but not impossible.

I turn back to the round mouth of the cave, barely taller than I am. I've got to seal it off somehow. I look at my free hand. I sure hope I can do this.

I press my palm to the rock wall of the cave and think of my poor, precious Hunter lying dead in the palace. The ice flows from my fingertips, circles up and around the mouth of the cave. Icicles grow out like teeth, reaching toward each other. They touch at the center and spread until the entire mouth of the cave is closed by a smooth window of ice. I continue to let the ice flow out of me, my body tiring, until it grows thick and white, no longer transparent. I drop my arm, exhausted. There. We should be safe for now.

I walk toward the little door at the bottom of the tower. I'm so tired. Now that I think about it, why didn't I let the Dwarves kill me? Why did running seem like the better idea? I am forever an outcast now. And my childhood is over.

I wrench open the stiff wooden door and turn in with the baby. Before shutting the door, I look at the green meadow around me, the fringe of trees and scruffy bushes, and the blocked mouth of the cave that leads down to the world I once knew.

We can never go back.

Chapter 37

My heart is frozen.

Hunter had given warmth to my life. I grew and blossomed under the sunshine of his love. Losing him is like losing the sun. I will never be warm again.

Night has fallen on this accursed kingdom. I'm standing at the window in the highest room of the tower. I listened while the Dwarves crashed through The Wood, searching for me. They didn't find me, not today. But they'll keep looking. I must thicken the ice, fill the whole cave with it if I can. I want to be completely alone.

The baby grunts behind me, reminding me I'm not alone. She's sleeping in the crate I stuffed with my old white dress. I was able to feed her – oh my *stars*, it hurt – and my tears fell on her face as she suckled. It scared me, how Godnutter just snatched the other baby from me. What if she comes back for this one? What if someone else does? This child is the only family I have left. I must keep her hidden, keep her safe. No one will ever steal her away from me. My little sister.

I decided to call her Rapunzel.

I spread my fingers on the stone ledge of the window. With some concentration, I spread a slick layer of ice over the sill. I raise my hands to rub the sting of chill out of them. Despite everything, I'm tempted to smile.

I have *power* now.

I don't have to feel small and helpless anymore. I don't need to be protected by anyone. I have magic, and it's strong. Undeveloped, of course - I need to practice. But I have lots of time ahead of me. I will grow this magic to fearful heights. Until I can freeze the whole kingdom if I choose. It's what they deserve.

I can't see much beyond the window. But out there in The Wood, Cinderella is still lying on her table, with no one to kiss her awake. Out there in The Wood, the seven Dwarves are hunting for my head. And out there in The Wood, there is no Hunter waiting for me at the well.

I blink and two tears slip onto my cheeks. I freeze them and they fall like diamond droplets, plinking when they hit the sill.

'Who are you, Snow White?' my mother asked, so contemptuously. As if I were nothing without her. I lift my chin and glare at the darkness. I don't need her or anyone else. I know who I am now.

I am the Snow Queen.

Coming Next:

Rotten Rapunzel

Join the Mailing List to receive updates and alerts when the next book is released.

http://www.anitavalleart.com/mailinglist.html

About the Author

To me it makes perfect sense that Snow White would become the Snow Queen. I mean, they've both got 'Snow' in their names, right? It had to happen sooner or later.

If it seems that this story has kind of a sad ending, all I can say is, hang in there. These characters will appear again and their stories will continue. Lots of fun and surprises ahead, so stay tuned! Make sure you sign up for the Royal Reader List so you don't miss the next book when it comes out. And if you like adult coloring books, I'm planning to draw a few scenes from *Sinful*

Cinderella and this book, and send them out free to subscribers. So sign up and you'll get them!

So about me, I grew up in Philadelphia, PA, but I live near Poughkeepsie, NY now. I've got four awesome siblings, two brothers and two sisters, who are my best friends in the whole world. When I'm visiting Philly, we all go out to dinner and call it our 'Sibling Supper.' And though most of us are in our 30s now, we still occasionally play Nintendo together. Some things you never grow out of!

If you enjoyed *Sneaky Snow White*, I'd be so grateful if you'd write a review for me on Amazon. You'd be surprised at how important reviews are, they make all the difference in the world. Books that get frequent reviews are bumped up higher on Amazon and get seen by more people. So it helps me out tremendously.

Thanks so much for supporting an indie author. God bless you.

-Anita Valle

Books by Anita Valle

Maelyn: The Nine Princesses –1
Coralina: The Nine Princesses –2
Heidel: The Nine Princesses –3
Briette: The Nine Princesses -4
Sinful Cinderella
The Bully Monster
50 Princesses Coloring Book
The Best Princess Coloring Book
Dog Cartoons Coloring Book

For more information, please visit my website:
http://www.anitavalleart.com
or e-mail me: **anitavalleart@yahoo.com**

Printed in Great Britain
by Amazon